Legend of the Huskahs

Secrets of the Merkabah

For Terry

Hamza Lawal

Hamza Lawal

Table of Contents

Dedication

This book is dedicated to the loving memory of a teacher who taught. It is also dedicated to all those who ask questions.

About the Author

Hamza Lawal is just a guy who woke up one day and decided to start oil painting and drawing. He also discovered that he enjoys writing fiction, and so decided to write. This will likely not be his only book. You can find out more about him and his work on instagram: @fiction_hamza.

Chapter 1: Mopti

The afternoon was incredibly chilled for the time of year, even though the wet season had not yet arrived. In the background, the sweet sounds of the kora —a musical instrument— played on. The music was giving a surreal touch to the scene under the blinding brightness of the Malian sun gradually becoming obscured by clouds befouled by Saharan sands as it furthered its descent, creating a resplendent glow on the horizon.

Mopti was a small settlement that lay on the Eastern Plateau, a day's journey northwest of the village of Bandiagara. All around me were traders and villagers rounding up on their daily activities before the call to evening rituals in a village mostly populated by Fula and Bozo people. I looked around with the wondrous eyes of a child, lost in imagination, soaking my surroundings in, but my concentration soon reached its demise. I was suddenly pulled back to reality by a kind voice that I had grown familiar with over the last few years.

"Let them bring you more food, Perig," said Samu, who had kindly agreed to bring me that far.

"No thanks, I've already eaten a lot," I refused rather politely. Samu sat on the floor with his legs folded and his back against the wall of a house made of mud with a thatched roof. Traditionally, most houses in the village bore that style, though if one were to venture farther west, towards the direction of the Empire's seat of government, Timbuktu, the affluence began to show in the buildings. That entire area was under the Mansa rulers, and they had then recently set out to create a wall extending from the western extremities of the continent of Bilad Asudan, all the way to the north-east. The Mansa rulers had a powerful army, and the soldiers enjoyed authority, respect, and stature. Samu glanced at me. I noticed his hair was greying as he was at least fifty years of age. Despite his age, he was still very young at heart. He was very tall, quite strong, with bulging eyeballs and had a wide frame. He said, "Do you know why they are creating a wall?" before I could respond, he continued, "they are trying to keep outsiders from disturbing those who lie in slumber."

Four years ago, before I embarked on the journey, I was told about a man who was considered a bit of a mystic in town. He did seem to know a lot of things, but he had once slipped and told me that he had studied at a university in Timbuktu and that many of the things he said were educated guesses and academic projections. "Do you know that one day, the walls will be completed, but they will be destroyed by invaders from the North, who will plunder and destroy all that has been built by the Empire?"

I stared at Samu and appeared to be lost but in agreement with him. I had no way of knowing if that would really happen, as it was common knowledge that the Mansa rulers had received powerful stone melting technology from the ancients, so it was inconceivable to me that such a thing could ever be a reality. That reminded me of my purpose of leaving my homeland and getting on the journey.

My guide, Samu, stood up and washed his face with water. He took another look at me and said, "I am going to say a little prayer because the sun has now set." He smiled gently and brought a small black cube out of his bag and placed it in front of him. He then stood up and circumambulated the cube seven times while uttering chants under his breath, almost inaudible. Moments later, he bowed twice facing the cube and then sat down motionless for about three minutes. Finally, he turned his head from right to left, saying, "Peace be upon all and the mercy of God be upon all too."

I extended my arm and shook his hand, and thanked him for the prayer.

"You'll have to teach me this one day, Samu," I said.

"Certainly, one day indeed," he replied. "As for now, let me tell you something that will become of the world in the coming years," said Samu with evident profundity.

"Go on please, I like listening to you, Samu," I responded, with a slight touch of excitement in my voice.

"A time will come when some humans will band together for political power. They will then rob people of their ability to communicate with the God within." Samu seemed to have a frown as he concentrated on what he was saying. He reached over to a corner and picked up a little kettle and placed it on a wire gauze, under which was a small flame. After a surreptitious glance at me, he asked if I would like some tea, I nodded in the affirmative, and he carried on.

"Our beloved Empire would have fallen then, and our legal books of law and morality which we call the 'books to be read' or the *qurans* will be edited and converted into dogmatic books."

"Wow! It was already the case in Britain and most of Europa. Our Druidic law is no more," I thought to myself. Samu reached over and grabbed a moringa stem which he placed in boiling water, and said, "What are you thinking about, young Perig?" I told him what I thought, and he said,

4

"everything happens in cycles, and I shall tell you all about the Mountain Tunnels and the possibility of the existence of that which you seek."

When he revealed to me that he was going to tell me about the Mountain Tunnels, I almost choked on the tea that I was drinking, out of a combination of shock and excitement. Four years ago, I left my homeland of Britain around the time that the Carta Mercatoria was written. The charter's aim was to grant foreign merchants even more freedom which would further cause the dwindling population of the Britons. About 800 years ago, many Angles, Saxons and Jutes arrived from across the sea and displaced my people, and now we were a minority. I initially travelled to the Empire because of my love for adventure and because I had lost the zeal to remain in Britain. However, when I arrived, I found that Samu had sustained a head injury during a hunting expedition, and so he became amnesiac, remembering only things that had happened thirty years ago. I wasn't going to leave, though. I used the opportunity to travel around and get familiar with the landscapes as well as the tribes around.

**

It was deep into the night, the weather was getting slightly chilly, and the fragrant smell of burnt bushes still lingering in the air. Samu gestured that I followed him into the house. In the midst of all that, a soothing warm, humid breeze from the south blew in my face, and I could hear some villagers in the background jubilating and rejoicing in grace as they perceived the breeze an early sign of the arrival of rainy season, or the tropical maritime air mass —as I had heard some people referring to it there—. My bed was made in the corner around ten feet from where Samu's was and I retired for the night.

"I have regained my memory, my friend!" The words rang in my ear for a few seconds after being awoken by Samu from my sleep. He sat up on his mattress excitedly.

"Thank goodness, Samu!" I replied.

"Yes, but something else has been revealed to me. It will not be possible for you to travel to the Mountain Tunnels unless you strengthen yourself." He looked at me reflectively and continued, "I am not talking about physical strength. I am talking about the strength of your inner vibrations, as we shall encounter forces you have never experienced before, in this our embarkation." At that point, I must have appeared puzzled, and upon seeing my expression, Samu said, "Words, thoughts and the mind in general casts an inaudible sound that permeates through everything. When allowed to prolong, it creates a reverberation. This, in turn, causes events and objects to appear. So over time, if you have allowed fear, consternation or any other emotion or thought

6

which is unlovely to linger in your mind, it will eventually cause certain events to take a turn for the 'negative', and I use that word loosely."

"Can you break it down, Samu? I think you are simply talking about being positive, as opposed to being a complete killjoy, right?" I asked my guide Samu. I did not know how that could cause events to take a turn for the worse, though, well, I supposed negativity could cause one to lose concentration. Samu smiled and said, "Go back to sleep and at first light, we shall be on our way."

***

The morning was far advanced by the time I was awakened by the bleating "Maa, maa" of a goat, right in my face. "*What happened,*" I thought to myself, *"and how did I end up sleeping this long?"* I immediately sprang to my feet in the old house. It was at least the second quarter of the morning. The windows were dusty and, although completely shut or closed, still let a shimmering light through. It was a bright morning. The echoing voices of young boys repeating prayers in unison penetrated the silence in the room and with the sounds of the streams gushing outside, collectively forming a mild melodic murmur. *"Exquisite,"* I thought.

I made my way outside and looked around, and found Samu under a mango tree, speaking to the town's people. He motioned for me to approach him. I hurriedly made my way, noticing a black bull being slaughtered not too far from where Samu was standing.

"In the dead of night, the thieves and vagabonds that they are, kidnapped a young woman and three children. They are slave traders," said a young man who was speaking to Samu. "Every year around this time, we have at least two or three cases in the delta. They usually travel south on the Bani River, though sometimes they travel north toward the Sahara." The young man was not shaken up at all by what had happened. He seemed angry and had a willing look to avenge.

Mopti used to be just a collection of huts, just a tiny hamlet, but at the time, there were at least 300 people living there. Though if that were a sign of things to come, then the auguries for its future was certainly not propitious. Saddened as I was about what transpired during the night, I reminded Samu of the urgency of our departure, to which he responded by saying, "You need to get something to eat; go to the room. I left some *yassa* for you inside a pot."

"Oh, I will. Thanks for that," I said.

I had paid Samu one pound and a silver penny— ceiniog— or denarius when I arrived four years ago, although he refused to accept it. He said his hospitality could only be repaid by God. He then instructed his wife to keep it safe for me until I was ready to return. To be fair, Samu lived in Timbuktu in an affluent quarter and was greatly respected, so he probably had little use for what I could afford. He, like me, derived great thrill from the adventure the life of exploration can offer.

"I must admit the *yassa* was delicious," I said to Samu as he entered the sitting room of the house that I had found him staying in. Samu decided to stay there in Mopti after his hunting accident so that he could recover but his wife was still in Timbuktu.

"Do you still have pygmies in Great Britain?" asked Samu while seeming to chortle a little with a slight smirk on his face.

"Yes, but they are mostly in lesser Britain now and are very few," I replied.

"There are still many here across the lands," he said in an impassioned way. "The small people have immense *magick* if they are trained, of course, and we will need the help of some of them on this journey!" Samu explained.

"Yes, there are many stories about them in the Isles, you know, about their abilities," I muttered and looked at Samu in agreement.

"When I was a young man, about your age, I went to a monastery in Syria and there, they didn't care what one's religion was or ethnic background, and I was treated very fairly despite the growing belligerence toward us Hebrews

9

in the current climate," Samu recalled, "which reminds me, your Hebrew has improved a lot, Perig!"

"Well, I've had four years, and I've grown very close to a young lady in the nearby Hamlet who has taken it upon herself a duty to make sure I'm fluent."

"Haha… I see you've been making good use of your time while I was regaining my memory," Samu laughed and then bemoaned but was content by how things unravelled for him. Samu was always grateful and seemed to be filled with *joie de vivre.*

"So as I was saying," he continued, "when I was at that monastery, I met a pygmy by the name of Suskup, and he had so many abilities, in fact, he graduated just after three months. Suskup was a Pygmy like no other I had ever seen. He had a lot in common with us, my dear boy. While you are of the last few of your kind, I myself, I'm the last of my kind with the blood of the Huskahs. Suskup was also the last of his kind." Samu concentrated on what he was saying.

"Just a quick interjection, Samu," I said, "aren't we leaving today?"

"We are," Samu replied with a sigh. "We just have to wait until the bull is prepared and fried for the orphans and the blind to eat. I have already washed the bull with the magical water of *Zam-Zam* and instructed the orphans to

10

recite the Holy names of God while taking a bite of the flesh of the bull."

"Where did you find the magical water?" I asked. Samu smiled, looking at a bowl of water inside a calabash.

He said, "Any water can be made holy. It is just like the *miqweh*. All you have to do is declare that it is now sanctified." Samu looked on into the calabash and carried on concentrating.

"You see, the Hebrew word *miqweh* simply means a collection. This is also the name of this village— Mopti. The word Mopti is in the Fulfulde language, and it means a collection or gathering. This is because the waters of the Niger and Bani rivers meet here, forming a delta, but symbolically speaking— and also since the founders of this town were esoterically inclined— the Mopti they meant, is the same as *miqweh* or *Zam-Zam* and so to that end, most of the waters here have been sanctified for centuries."

I looked at Samu in amazement, "Wow! Interesting," I commented. Samu then carried on, "At the time of Zuwa Al Yaman, who arrived in these regions over 600 years ago, founding the settlement of Kukiya, a powerful crystal was buried inside the Niger River in the town of Kukiya. Zuwa Al Yaman was exiled from Yemen —the fortunate land— when their king was defeated, and so, they ran away with the crystal and needed to hide it somewhere. And that is how it

11

ended up buried in the Niger River— at least that's what the legend says. These Hebrews then went on to found many towns across the lands; today, these lands are referred to as Bilad Asudan. Are you with me?"

My eyes trailed a little, and I scratched my head perplexedly. The information was all too intense and a little far-fetched. "I do understand what you are saying, Samu. But how can we find this crystal? And will the crystal help us get to the Mountain Tunnels? Also can I find stone melting tools ?" I asked a series of questions excitedly.

"Well, have you ever gone scuba diving?" he inquired with a laugh.

"There are no crocodiles, are there?"

"Don't worry about crocodiles," said Samu.

By then, it was late in the morning, the smell of fried beef ruling the air, the sun almost reaching its zenith, and the heat unrelenting. Orphans, the blind and the crippled gathered around, arriving to have a piece or two of the flesh of the beef and to get ready to say a prayer.

Samu gestured that I be given a few pieces of the beef but I received a whole bowl. I thought he was going to have some too, but he reminded me that I would need some for our journey and that he no longer consumed meat.

As the crowd of orphans began to disperse, I noticed a little girl sat near me, who went on to ask me why my hair was like the texture of thread. "And why are your eyes like this?" the little girl asked while touching the fringes of the carpet spread across the veranda, in her curiosity. Soon other kids arrived and started examining me closely. Though my skin was almost as dark as the people in the village, I had blue eyes —something of a rarity there— and straight wavy hair. My facial features were also quite different, and I had more of a robust framework, while the people there seemed to be rather lanky of stature. They could tell that I was a foreigner. It always amazed me how astute and observant children can be at times.

"I am from Britain," I said. "Some of us look like me." Samu then ordered the kids to leave, and I noticed he, too, looked at me as if he was seeing me for the first time.

He scolded the kids once more and then said, "Do you know that they've started breeding people again in certain parts of these lands?"

"Yes, it's very common in Europa," I replied. "In my homeland of Britain, only among the Britons and Welsh do you still find a few people like me that retain our dark complexion. Due to the selective breeding that is taking place, there are people with no touch of darkness anymore, particularly among the Anglo Saxons," I explained. "There are women that are now bred in Circassia, called the *Hur*, mainly for the purpose of concubinary. I heard that they are made to have certain features that are sought after by the highest bidders."

Samu stared into empty space almost hopelessly and then said, "Imagine the world we live in today. What is to become of us in future? There was a king that existed in a place southwest of Great Zimbabwe. The king bred women with extremely large posteriors and breasts and instructed all people to be nudists so that he could enjoy looking at women that appealed to him." Samu caught me smiling after he had said that, and in my defence, I joked, "Well, at least the king was only looking, not touching."

"Things change, my dear Perig. Many people will beg to differ today, when you mention to them that their breed came to proliferate as a result of some kind of fetish."

"Right, yes Samu," I answered. "Can I ask you a quick question before we leave?" Samu nodded, and I continued, "why is this continent referred to as the Black lands?"

Samu looked at me, grabbed a jar made with calabash, in which he had herbal tea, took a quick gulp and chewed on a *muruchi* fruit, and said, "Well, it isn't only this continent. There are so many countries around the world that named themselves after their appearance. You see, because of the birth of mercantilism and other exploitative systems of commerce, merchants only think of maximising profits at the expense of all moral apparatuses. They have now even opened a genetic Pandora's Box, whereby they are changing the very human nature in an effort to commercialise human beings. Not unlike how fruits and crops are commercialised to appeal to the less than honourable proclivities of men. I believe these lands are called by that name out of pride that they have maintained their unaltered complexions."

Chapter 2: The Crystal

"Pass me the rope! What is wrong with you? Do you want me to drown? Just twist it. I can't hold on alone! The current is too strong! Listen—"

"I am trying. I'm trying. I think the loop is no longer there. I told you guys the loop is not strong enough... but keep holding on to the canoe and I'll swim to shore and get Samu to hurl me a new rope. There is one with a loop!"

"Thaahs crazy! How do I keep the canoe in place without paddling?" I screamed back at Ali, a local resident of Gao who was helping me dive into the Niger River in the town of Gao to locate Samu's crystal.

"Samu, I think we can't find the crystal like this... the current is too strong," I yelled toward Samu, but he did not respond. Samu was seated by the shore in a lotus position with his eyes closed. At that moment, I let go of the canoe, and it drifted away downstream, eventually getting caught in a nearby meandering peatland. I took a huge inhalation and dived into the river, which was an experience like no other. The commotion was suddenly, contradictorily, silenced by the tranquillity inside the river. "*I know the River Niger in Gao is so crystal clear due to the mineral-rich soil, which has low porosity, but even so, it is too clear. There is something strange,*" I thought to myself as I thrust deeper. The riverbed was armoured by the most beautiful precious stones, many of which coruscated as they caught the light of the sun. Flora and fauna were everywhere. It was a whole world, teeming with life.

At the corner of my eye lay a shipwreck from centuries ago, I presumed. Once a thing of man but in her death and wreckage born anew—a belle of nature. Thousands of little fish swarmed the structure. The waters at the riverbed were cool, and among the wreckage was a metallic chest. I used my dagger to force the dowels open. Nestled within it was a small box, and inside the box was an empty slot. "*Perhaps it was used to store the crystal,*" I thought. I quickly resurfaced as fast as I could and returned to shore.

"Goodness, Samu, you are just seated here in gay abandon while we almost died, trying to locate the crystal," I said, and I could hear Ali chuckling.

"Huh? How do you think you were able to see underwater and hold your breath for thirty-odd minutes?" Samu retorted. "It is because of the powers of the amulet I gave you. You don't become superhuman after two days travelling on horseback —from Mopti to Gao— you know," he laughed.

"I didn't find anything down there, *there* was no crystal," I said, and I could see Ali looking disappointed too, as I was. Samu yawned, stretched his arms, stood up and then replied, "You did find something. I knew the crystal wasn't there. I did tell you that there is one in the town of Kukiya and not here. All I wanted you to find was the shipwreck. Did you see any inscriptions on it?

"Yes, I did. Written in Kufic script, I think it said Zeghe."

Samu looked impressed. "Good! Perig, now you have the ability to see underwater, and you can also hold your breath for thirty minutes. You see, the flesh of the sacrificial bull that you consumed two days ago, along with the amulet, has completed your training. If you recall, I did tell you that you were not strong enough to go to the Mountain Tunnels just yet." Ali and I looked at each other in utter bewilderment. *"Samu was a very complicated character indeed, but that must be his idea of a heuristic approach to learning, I guess,"* I thought to myself.

The rest of the day was uneventful. From our hilltop abode, I could see the whole town. Lamps in houses burned as night approached, creating a twilight glow above and below, with an area of darkness in the middle, demarcating the city of Gao into two distinct towns, coming together to form the city. The residents of the city were called *Burzurkaneen* and were very honest to the point of naïveté. There was a powerful ruler, feared even by the great Malian Empire. He was called the Qanda, or supreme ruler. The streets were full of prefects, patrolling with the aim of stifling political dissent. Rumours abounded that the Malian

18

Empire—which governed a territory larger than the whole of Western Europa— had sleeper cells in the city of Gao. So the security was even tighter. Treading cautiously, the Qanda did not even rule his subjects from the town of Saney, residing instead in a royal town, along with ministers and other trusted officials high in the echelons of power.

At a distance, flickering lights from lamps carried by the serried ranks of hundreds of marabouts in a procession along with smoke rising from the burning of ritualistic incense created a beautiful radiance that culminated in an illusion analogous to the murmuration of birds in flight. At the farthest recesses of the town, lined along the streets, were statuary made of marbles, glistening under the moonlight, making them pop out of the landscape. I was slightly disappointed that our efforts of finding the crystal yielded no fruits. *"Did we travel all the way from Mopti to Gao for nothing? Will we find it tomorrow?"* These were the thoughts that filled my head before sleep escaped with my awareness.

***

After the events at the River Niger, I wasn't prepared for any more surprises from Samu. We left the twin towns of Gao early the next evening and arrived at the town of Taadamakkah —a sacred valley— in the early hours of the morning.

"Gentlemen, this is Taadamakkah!" yelled Samu with a broad smile on his face. "Taadamakkah means 'this is Makkah' in the Berber language. It's mainly a religious centre; pilgrimage takes place here. Ehh!—" Samu mumbled as a locust flew into his mouth.

"Do you think the crystal is here, Samu?" I asked as we dismounted our horses, fastened them by a tree and walked into a nearby bazaar. Ali did not seem interested at all in the whereabouts of the crystal anymore. He instead ran into the market to find a repast. It seemed he was very hungry all along.

"Yes indeed, I'm sure there is a crystal here, and we are going to steal it, or rather you are." Samu seemed certain about the location of the crystal this time around.

We sat at a market stall and ordered some food. "Hmm... as long as the crystal can help get us to the Mountain Tunnels, it's worth a shot, I guess," I replied.

"Great, we shall go to the guests' quarters shortly to rest and then we will find the crystal under the cover of darkness, later on," Samu suggested.

The scene at the bazaar was memorable— sun-faded woollen fabric tarps sprung above rickety wooden stalls, goods from Marakesh, Granada, Cairo, Timbuktu, the Great Ghana and beyond, layered atop tables, and excited shopkeepers chanting and calling customers. The traditional bògòlanfini fabric from Timbuktu hung stall after stall while the shoppers swarmed ubiquitously. Some were sauntering as though out for a countryside ramble, while others were marching in haste as the bazaar raged on, while the sun continued its ascent in a blaze of glory.

21

At the back of the market was a landfill, the smell of which reached where we were sat ever so often. A rancid smell mixed with sweat, faeces and decay. The sour odour would have ruled the breathable air were it not for the fierce competition coming from the earnest burning of incense emanating from the city centre.

***

The town of Taadamakkah, had guest quarters just like most towns around there, where outsiders were allowed to stay free of charge, provided they did not exceed one night. At the centre of Taadamakkah was its capital Zakraam, where our guest quarter was located. I must have been out for a few hours after retiring, but when I awoke, both Samu and Ali were ready for us to start looking for the crystal. Samu motioned for Ali and I to follow him slowly outside the sleeping quarter and into the city.

The city was unique—the streets thirty-foot wide and laid out in geometric patterns adorned with an enchanting architecture, and raging grasslands, typical of the Sahel but more charming because acacia trees were specifically arranged along all walkways, creating an orderly expression. The streets were made of stone but not cobbled, rather of huge slabs. The stonework spoke the language of a bygone era. I recalled the moment I was at the riverbed of the Niger River at Gao. The armoured riverbed did not seem natural at all. Seeing the architectural prowess at Taadamakkah, it was not too hard to conclude that the riverbed must have been rubble or a rip-rap—meaning that it was man-made.

When we arrived at the city centre we saw a pyramidal structure at the centre of the ruins of an ancient concourse. It was made up of two pyramids, about the size of a small caravan. One was placed on the ground and the other inverted and placed on top, in a manner that they seemed to swallow each other. "What is this?" whispered Ali. It was clearly where all the incense was coming from. *The Marabouts evidently use this place for their processions,"* I thought to myself.

"This structure that you see here is the physical representation of a Merkabah. A Merkabah is simply a geometric motif," Samu explained in a hushed voice. "This place used to be a university where students were taught how to leave the physical body and travel in spirit, where time and space do not matter anymore. It is said that there, after travelling to the highest realms, one can see God or the inner nature of the mind where 'the ALL' comes from. I think the marabouts still use it for such teachings. All across Bilad Asudan are scattered sacred towns by the name of Makkah or Merka, which signify places where the secret, sacred teachings of Merkabah are held. Many *peregrinus* come here to learn every year. Aforetime, the teachings were kept hidden from the masses. It is for this reason that the Hismaic tongue still uses the term *haraam* —forbidden— and the word sacred interchangeably," Samu explained while looking at the structure as a broken stone stele on the ground caught his attention. He read both Kufic and Hebrew perfectly.

"Where are these teachings from?" I asked Samu.

"Oh! These teachings are as old as mam. In contemporary times, they were written in the language of Meroe, and Hebrew, translated from arcane languages, but now many translations are in Hismaic in this part of the world and in Latin and in the language of the Hellenes in Andalusia. My fear is that in the coming years, this information will be commercialised, like everything else. Man has a predilection to seek for vicarious saviours, so 'they' will exploit that tendency and create saviours and god-men by historicizing mythological archetypes." Elucidated Samu quite poetically and then located the crystal etched within the south side of the structure. I hurriedly armed myself with a dagger and vigorously began to try to remove the crystal from its socket while Ali worked on the opposite side as well, but our efforts were yielding no joy.

Samu began to cast a spell to soften the encasing rock so that the crystal could be removed easily. As he chanted louder and louder, the crystal began to move.

Ali's pupils dilated, and raged with excitement. He screamed, "I have never seen anything like this before!" Samu carried on as we all put in more and more effort. The crystal was almost out of its socket when all of a sudden, it was fastened back in place, and the whole episode came to an abrupt end— the marabouts were all around us, but instead of arresting us, they prostrated.

Chapter 3: The Old Mosque

Two weeks passed since the events at the ancient concourse-pyramidal temple where the crystal was, and now though not a captive, I felt myself imprisoned by circumstances. Here was I, unable to leave, unable to carry on with my quest due to being domiciled at a temple with the marabouts. The marabouts called it the Great Mosque of the Holy Sepulchre. An old mosque in a desolate quarter of Gao called Aljanabanbia, which I had no recollection of arriving at.

"These people were caught trying to steal the crystal at the Markabahallah," I heard one of the students saying as they passed by my room. *So that is what they call the pyramidal structure: Markaballah,"* I thought to myself. "They sent the other guy home, and this one is free to go, but they are keeping the older man," another student said as they dawdled past while touching the walls of the hallway.

The hallway that stood as a testament to the glorious days of the old mosque. It was built on a foundation of stone, but the walls were constructed with sun-baked earthen clays called *ferey*. Through the gaps of the bricks, a sand-based mortar could be seen. Once covered in plaster, which would have given the walls a smooth and polished look, now wilted like crusted scabies. The walls had certainly seen better days. On the exterior of the walls toward a large courtyard, a display of visible scaffolding made with deleb palms called *toron*, one after another, creating a phantasmagoric arrangement of shadows that casts an artistic display at certain times of the day—bringing the huge stone stelae which adorn the courtyard, to life.

Toward the direction of an underground chamber were marabouts googly-eyed and acting secretive as they paced back and forth, as if they did not want the students to know what was going on or what they kept there.

"Where is my friend, Samu, who I was travelling with? They told me I could see him. Since yesterday" I asked two acolytes as they paced past me. "Why are you ignoring me?" I queried.

"Master Samu is needed here, please be patient, and you are free to go anyway," said one of the acolytes with a confused but stern look on his face. I grabbed the acolyte by the forelock and asked again. He shrieked and shuddered and then gestured toward a door. Without contemplation or hesitation, I barged into a medium-sized hall, and I saw Samu seated on a chair while a tube was inserted into his arm. Around him at least a dozen marabouts. They were drawing his blood.

"Samu, are you okay?" I yelled. Samu glanced at me and said he was fine. "We are just conducting experiments here,

Perig." He looked drained and fatigued. He sighed, removed the tube from his arm and struggled to stand on his feet.

"The experiments have failed, anyway, gentlemen. Sorry I wasn't of much help," Samu staggered as he leapt on, eventually making his way toward the door.

"Wait, Samu!" called out a loud and powerful voice from the back of the chamber. "You HAVE been of great help to us here during your stay." An old man emerged from the shadows, very tall of stature with greyish-black skin, silvery hair, deep sunken eyes and a propulsive gait caused by his bent spine under the weight of years.

"Please, have a seat, regain your strength before you leave," the old man instructed. Samu agreed, and we both sat down on a row of benches that formed concentric circles around the chamber. "You've all heard about the Holy Sepulchre," the old man continued. "Well, this is the Holy Sepulchre. For years we have awaited the coming of someone who has a trace of the blood of the Huskahs, and you came right to us, Samu." The old man explained while directing a basket of fruits consisting of mangoes, dates, jujube, weda and hanza fruit to be given to us.

At the centre of the room, not too far from where Samu was seated, was a stone sarcophagus and within it a mummy. "Behold the last of the full blooded Huskahs, lays here dead, no more! Returned to the great beyond. You are blessed,

28

Samu, to have perhaps a quarter of the blood of the Huskahs," the old man reiterated for what seemed like the fourth or fifth time as he pointed at the mummy. The mummy was laid in a shallow sarcophagus, with its arms crisscrossed.

"Knoweth yond the life of this w'rld is m'rely a game and a div'rsion and ostentation and a causeth of boasting 'mongst yourselves and trying to outdo one anoth'r in wealth and children: liketh the plant-growth aft'r raineth which delights the cultivat'rs, but then t with'rs and thee seeth t turning yellow, and then t becomes broken stubble. In the next w'rld th're is t'rrible punishment but eke f'rgiveness from God and his valorous pleasure. The life of this w'rld is nothing but the enjoyment of delusion." The old man read an engraving on the side of the sarcophagus. Though it appeared as if he did not actually read it, then and there, but rather recalled from memory as his eyesight seemed to be very poor.

"I'm certain the sarcophagus is from Makuria. The inscriptions are in the language of Meroe," sputtered Samu as he enjoyed a weda fruit. He seemed to be getting his strength back. *"Poor guy, how long was he intending to keep giving them his blood",* I thought.

"…basically that engraving on this sarcophagus is as our great old torahs and qurans –books of law– say. In this short

29

peregrination we call life, would you rather have the experience of a pigeon or an eagle? Would you rather see the world through the eyes of a lion or that of a gazelle? It is simply in this spirit that we drew your blood, of course, with your consent, Samu...." The old man then leapt off back into the shadows from whence he came.

**

We left the Mosque of the Holy Sepulchre where the body of the last Huskah lay and headed out on a boat on the Niger River toward the direction of the ancient city of Kukiya.

"That place gives me the creeps," I said, and Samu nodded in agreement. "Why were you letting them draw out your blood anyway?" I asked with a sigh.

"They won't find anything in my blood, and I had to pretend to cooperate with them. Otherwise, things would have got ugly. They weren't going to take no for an answer," Samu said, looking decidedly upset. "We have to find another way to get a similar crystal. There is another one at Kukiya, and we must get it. Local legend says, a long time ago, the crystals fell from the sky and contain great power. Without that, we cannot go to the Mountain Tunnels," Samu said as we boarded a boat.

The boat was part of a small fishing fleet that had launched from Timbuktu, painted in stripes of lime-green, orange, and white. The mast, adorned with good luck charms poked into the dusky afternoon sky—which was laden with cloud cover—. While the sail hung loose to the deck. The crew were only five in number and consisted of a diver, three fishermen and their captain. It was a short journey south from Gao to Kukiya. The captain looked at me suspiciously and said, "You are not from around here, are you?" with a slight grin on his face.

"No!" I replied. "Is that a problem?" Samu looked at me as if to say the captain had it coming.

"No, no, no, not a problem at all, ahhaff... I'm just trying to say—"

"What are you trying to say exactly?" Samu interrupted the captain before he could finish.

"Well, you know... that clearly our kind—Hebrews— aren't necessarily welcome up north, and he's from somewhere there," the captain retorted while looking at his companions for support, to which they gave without holding their tongues. "Yes, that's true, those miserable northerners," yelled the diver.

"Listen, I came here because I thought this was sanctuary. The land of the free? My kind isn't wanted up north either. That's why I came here. I heard the king of Gao even pretends to be a Muhammadan in public but isn't really, behind closed doors. Who knows what his real beliefs are?"

31

I addressed all the fishermen and finally got them to nod in approval. "Whose kind are wanted anywhere anyway, these days," interjected one of the fishermen with a large stomach and strong palms that had been roughened by years of labour.

"Well, I'm glad someone finally agrees with me," I replied.

The fisherman then sipped on a traditional palm wine called *chimichama* and continued, "My people used to be slaves, captured by the Tuareg and forced to work for no fault of ours. Other than that, we are few and unable to defend ourselves."

Before the dawn of evening, we approached the mysterious city of Kukiya. I had heard so much about the city, so naturally, I was eager to see what it had to offer. With inquisitive eyes, I began to examine the environs, keenly comparing them to the legendary stories of beauty, magic and wealth that I had heard. As we left the shores of the Niger River, I realised that the city was but a shadow of its past. The glorious old days that built the legends were evidently long gone, as rubble after rubble were all that we were presented with. "Samu, this is not what I've heard about this place," I said to my guide and friend Samu, who was neither as surprised as me nor as bothered about what became of Kukiya. "The city was destroyed by the Malian

Empire in the early days of its march eastward. It is said that the city was ruled by a queen who resisted all attempts at diplomacy from Timbuktu," Samu replied while unloading his travel belongings. He sat down on the ground, stretched his tired legs and continued, "This place is centuries older than the temples at Meroe. It was in an epoch more ancient, in an antiquity without date, that their beliefs were formed, and their religion and culture were birth. That culture still exists here. So I'd tread with caution if I were you!" Samu muttered with a yawn as he seemed about to doze off.

"Classic Samu, you just say something like that and just go to sleep, just under the tree, without any worry in the world."

***

Still, my curiosity was not quenched, dissatisfied with Samu's advice, and with a morbid curiosity, I left him to take a nap while I went for a walk around the city. The city was well irrigated by canals that penetrated every nook and cranny like capillaries, masterfully built with the impressive megalithic architecture of the ancient world. "*I have seen the likes of these in Venice, although these seem older and more decrepit and also show signs of being quarried and used as spolia,*" I thought to myself. Then the rubbles I had seen earlier made sense. It was evident that scavengers were mining the city for its very last spoils of war.

The city was without the growing aridity ever creeping on the northern cities of the Empire, but still, I felt the dry winds of the north and saw the intense fine sands of the Sahara rested upon the window stools of countless buildings mixed with moisture carried by the more humid air—creating a haven for mildew, earthy scents of moist dirt and an overgrowth of carnivorous shrubbery.

Around me were the imposing remains of hallowed out temples with broken statuary, made faceless by the withering of time, crumbling staircases and caved-in roofs under the weight of scandent vines. There were also collapsed walls of the ancient city and fallen battlements riddled with blade marks. Rustling sounds could be heard under dried leaves from small animals such as agama lizards and rats that had long overrun the temples. In contrast, there were other buildings maintained to some degree, and also some laundry hung across walls, which indicated human habitation. One of the houses had a large African locust bean tree —locally known as *néré*— I moved closer to that house as I heard footsteps, hoping it was not a dangerous animal.

"Shhh, don't be too loud. Remember, no one knows we are working here!" I suddenly heard a barely audible sentence in a hushed voice, carried over to my ears by a calm breeze. I carefully climbed a fallen wall covered by mounds of soil and, lo and behold, marabouts snooping around and instructing their students. The marabouts were at the altar of an old synagogue or temple, digging. I knew it was the same marabouts from the old mosque or at least from the same order because they were wearing the same washed-out blue clothes with the same insignia on the bodice or front part of the garb. I had to let Samu know.

Chapter 4: A Night without End

As night approached, another side of the town that lay dormant under the glare of the sun and the priggish eyes of sanctimonious priest awoke. Under the blanketing embrace provided by the darkness of night, as she spread her dark shrouds over the city, chants and drums reigned, and alcohol was the order of the day. Suddenly, the anonymity of darkness brought forth a new revelrous order. It was a scene of bacchanalia like I had never known.

There was a large bonfire, and people were out dancing, drinking and laughing. I decided to make my way to the bonfire, treading through ancient alleyways that were disused and careful not to stumble on any overhanging or low hanging branches or algae forming on rocks. Soon, I approached a part of the city that seemed more habitable, as the sounds of laughter, drums, the kora musical instrument and even *zaghareet* or ululation, and chants grew louder and louder, creating an unpleasant cacophony.

"This must be the place I saw earlier—from a distance— with signs of human habitation," I thought to myself while I continued to explore the scene, being thankful for the full moon that had now appeared with illuminating radiance after the torrential clouds dispersed.

There were women of all ages naked from behind but covered on the front side by a huge mask that hung as low as their navels, though some were bare-chested with smaller masks, but not a single woman was without a mask. "Here you go, honey! Wear a mask. No ordinary humans allowed here," said a middle-aged woman, who left her group as she handed me over a tribal mask. "There are no other masks left. You'll have to be a *Usetorohila* tonight or wait until next year. And get naked, please, uuh! No one is supposed to be with clothes. Kill the ego," she said with a playful but disgruntled tone of voice, hastening to catch up with her group.

I could hear another group chanting in unison, "You'll not hear the music of *Donsoton* here because they say women cannot be hunters, and women cannot go on their hunting expeditions. Therefore they are not allowed here. If you are a *Donsoton*, tonight, you lose your identity or die! Oho oho oho no *Donsoton*." The group chanted as they dispersed into a larger crowd, heading in the direction of the bonfire. The *Donsonton* were hunters but also musicians that performed in one of the oldest surviving forms of music that existed in the Empire or perhaps even the entire Bilad Asudan.

After taking a narrow alleyway, I arrived at a hall with broken tables, calabash bottles on the floor —some half-empty—, music playing, moans of joy emerging from darker corners that I did not care to explore further, as well as some moans of indignation and pain, and the unmistakable smell of hashish.

The hall opened out to where the bonfire was. People were walking up and down, and everyone was going about their business. I noticed that some of the masked people were not all women. They were men and boys— also naked.

A high pitched voice called out for all to be silent, and all drumming came to an end. Except for the occasional mummers and giggles here and there, it was still and noiseless.

"Quiet all! And show respect to the queen of the night, the goddess of freedom, the mother of the wronged, and the provider of security." The voice commanded. There was a parade of boys that ran across and formed a semi-circle around a doorway with lamps agleam. From within the opening emerged the queen that was introduced earlier, and the high pitched voice announced again, "welcome our mother, Queen Mi-nana."

The queen was naked, clothed only by gold ornamentations and a thin veil across her waist. Her solferino-red hair was coiled, spiralling upward to the sky like something out of an ophidian nightmare, but embellished and anchored by a golden crown of the most precious gems, glistening under the moonlight and the light of the bonfire.

The queen had a broad collar necklace, bracelets and bangles on her wrist and ankles with a keen and peculiar family crest. I tried to get closer to have a look at the crest but was stopped by guards that did not seem to be partaking in the intoxication. The queen's mask was not made of wood like that of the revellers but was instead made of glass and only covered half her face while the lower part was not covered so that she could eat and drink to her heart's content without having to move the mask.

By then, I was close enough to observe the high pitch voiced announcer, and upon close examination, he appeared to be a castrato or eunuch. It then became clear that even the boys and the other men that I had seen earlier were all castratos. *"Could it be that the woman who gave me the mask thought I was a eunuch too? Is that why she told me to get naked. Are there only eunuchs here? I got to find Samu,"* puzzled, I queried myself in thought.

As I struggled through crowds, I caught a glimpse of someone that could be Samu but lost him in the commotion. I then realised I was dehydrated after not drinking any water all evening. Reaching a table, I grabbed a calabash full of fresh water from a nearby well and quenched my thirst. Now I was in a better position to find Samu but as I settled on that idea and began looking for Samu, I was approached by a young man who offered me a huge skewer of mutton, mixed with garden eggs, prepared in an open flame– that I could not resist.

After my meal, there was a short speech by the queen in which she said, among other things, "I am Queen Mi-nana, saviour of the wronged. This night is a night of many rites. Please enjoy yourselves and remember that our numbers will continue to grow, and they will never get rid of our old ways." The queen said, and then gently sat on her throne.

Four men then emerged from the crowd, naked from head to toe —except for the masks which they donned—. The men were holding a golden arc. The announcer then introduced them, "Behold! The arc of the covenant!" he said, pointing at the arc, as the four men placed it inside a huge green coloured cuboid structure near the bonfire. "The arc of the covenant that houses our precious stone," the announcer continued, "and now it's time for the procession of Children of Daud and Yonotan."

The four men that placed the golden chest in the green cuboid structure then began to dance in a choreographed fashion, they started canoodling, and moments later, lascivious activities ensued. In the midst of that, other men from the Children of Daud and Yonatan group joined in until the group reached a size of at least thirty individuals. I was completely awestruck by what I had just witnessed but it seemed all too normal to the attendees.

"The night is still young! I now call upon the Children of Saris to come and give us a display of their performance," said the high pitch voiced announcer. Right away, a crowd of young boys assembled and began to march in a military fashion, soon to be joined by men and women who fancied them. This display went on for quite a lot longer than that of the previous group.

Finally, the announcer called out for the Children of Usetorohila to conglomerate for their procession. It was then that I recalled that the lady who gave me the mask said I belonged to this group. I then noticed that the design of each mask represented the group it belonged to.

I tried to remain in the crowd by walking toward a cluster of people to avoid joining the processions, but I was hurled out violently. "No, not a chance; everyone must join in the fun," yelled a man and a woman as they pushed me to join the Children of Usetorohila that I apparently belonged to.

The processions involved moving around in circles with a partner, and as I joined, I was pulled by a tall woman with a delicate but sinewy figure. "Why are you moving funny? Is it your first time?" she asked.

"Yeah, I'm new here," I replied. My head was awhirl from all the moving around. "I don't feel too well," I screamed so that she could hear me, but my voice sounded muffled.

"Alright, why don't you sit down over there," she said and led me to a corner away from the crowds. "You can rest for a while and come back and join the rites later. People rest all the time. You don't have to do everything all at once if you are tired," she added, turned around and trotted off briskly— revealing her athleticism. Lost in thought, I kept my eyes on her until she disappeared into the crowd.

**

Moments later, the announcer called out for the queen's grand priest. The entire gathering was quiet upon the arrival of the priest, who was covered in charms, amulets and talismans of different sizes. Intrigued, I moved closer to the bonfire as people seemed unduly obsequious. The priest was frail of stature, had a shaven head and very thin fingers, his face carefree, with a full beard. The priest then began to repeat the words 'bor, bor, bor, bor!' and then started to quiver in a convulsive manner. Twisting and turning on the ground, he stood up, "Kimari, Nama, Riti, Kauneka, Dicha, Tayyar, Mbiwiri! Come forth our seven ancestral spirits," he yauped loudly.

In a cloud of smoke, the first jinn emerged, and then, like a small tornado, it stirred up dust and nearly put out the bonfire, to which people gasped in fright and awe. One by one, all seven spirits materialised as the priest continued to evoke them. Some were like lurid flames but smokeless, while others moved like wraiths or spectres. The fifth jinn was Dicha, a beautiful woman with unhumanly large eyes and hoofed legs. As clear as day, visible to the blind and audible to the deaf, I saw and heard these creatures. Eventually, the priest commanded the spirits to depart, and

43

they converged into a luminous- floating orb and moved heavenwards, mesmerisingly so, as if taking the soul of the gathering— they vanished. I was absolutely stunned by what I had just witnessed.

The announcer then spoke again, this time commanding people to circumambulate the green coloured cuboid structure that contained the 'arc of the covenant', and people began to march around the cuboid structure. "This is the purest of all tabernacles," said the announcer. As if under some enchanting compulsion, I joined the ritual. "This is our closing ritual, and this marks the end of this year's rites," continued the announcer.

The crowd that was going around the cuboid structure was the biggest group task throughout the night. Now everyone was partaking, including the queen, who was carried in a palanquin by four strong men. People's bodies —now without masks— rubbed against each other tightly in a carousel of sweat and debauchery. I staggered on and on among the people of the town going around the cuboid structure. I was very tired, I felt my eyelids were heavy and my feet numb. Suddenly, as if in an attempt at escapism, I drifted high up in the sky. Looking down, I could see my poor body among hundreds of people, moving involuntarily like a zombie while I floated in the clouds. I could see the whole town from up there and the bonfire. The crowd below looked like a colony of ants while the clouds— a humid utopia. I could see migratory birds in flight and the River Niger glowing under the moonlight. The sensation was truly liberating, but the experience was fleeting. Weightlessly, like a leaf, I descended until I returned to my body in the crowd.

Not long after, the crowds began to disperse, and I heard a familiar voice saying, "Look who I found. Hello Perig, looks like you've been having fun," it was Samu, with two women who had their arms wrapped around his waist. "Samu, where have you been? You can't believe what happened, the type of things that I saw," I replied, but Samu just smiled and addressed the women, "It was a pleasure meeting you lovely ladies, and please have a wonderful night." The ladies waved at us and walked away, and he turned around and looked at me with a cynical grin, saying, "I warned about their ancient ways."

Chapter 5: Toloy Inhumation

"So, are we not going to talk about that night at Kukiya at all, Samu? Whenever I mention it, you just brush it off as if it's nothing."

"Hmm, are you talking about that dog and pony show, Perig?"

"Oh, don't be so cynical, Samu. Everybody saw those spirits. It was very real." I replied, looking at Samu intently as if to say: 'seriously?'

"No, it wasn't real at all. It's all just an elaborate hoax performed by a puppeteer; so-called priest. What you guys saw, or rather what you thought you saw, was smoke and mirrors. Besides, keep this in mind, everything there was laced with '*Iboga*' which is a powerful hallucinogen. Did you eat or drink anything?"

"Yes, I drank some water and had a little something en brochette. You might be right... So are you trying to say jinns are not real?" I asked while having an internal debate, "*could I have been deceived?*"

"No, I'm not saying that. What they call jinns are simply just your thoughts. Thoughts can be created to have a purpose, to have a birth date, and one can breathe life into them and so on and so forth. Let's say, as an example, you want to find a missing item. You may imagine an entity charged with the responsibility of locating that item."

46

"Ok, that could make sense, but how does the entity bring the item to you without having a physical body?" I asked as the rays of the sun pierced through the cracks of the small wooden window of a riverside cafe, blinding Samu momentarily. We stopped at the cafe for refreshments on the way out of the town of Kukiya.

"If you concentrate hard and consistently enough"... he paused for effect "...through visualisations and rituals, the created being can be strong enough to lead you to the item. Otherwise, it may come as dreams or even as messages in people's conversations —even strangers—."

"So, what if the creature takes a mind of its own?"

"Well, that depends on your intended purpose and the amount of energy you can put into your creation. Great mages of yonder could even make creatures that had the ability to bring to them what they wanted. Nonetheless, care must be taken not to create a nithing. So when tired or moody, never attempt any of this, especially without years of erudition." Samu explained, and a sigh of gratification followed.

"Interesting, so in that case, is God the same thing?" I asked, being sure that Samu would answer in the affirmative.

"Not exactly, but let's talk about God or what *they* think God is another time. For now, we need to get ready. A long journey awaits us."

47

I had my doubts about what Samu said. I know that what I saw in Kukiya —that godforsaken town—was not some presentation. "Samu, there is something else that happened. While circumambulating that green cube, I left my body for a while. I was high up in the sky, floating."

"That's what Ibogaine is capable of causing. Basically, you had a herb-induced out-of-body experience. Now you have the ability to perform aerial surveillance. We just have to figure out the right dose of Ibogaine," Samu said in jest.

***

We left the town of Kukiya early in the morning and arrived at the town of Mopti in the evening, which was in a state of pandemonium— huge flames swallowing thatched roofed houses while dark smokes belched harrowingly, blinding and intoxicating. There was a raid from the north— part of a series of attacks—likely by the Beni Hassan tribes that roam the far reaches of the Sahel. Displaced by desertification, they have become hardened by circumstances and now don the garb of warriors. Although, there were rumours circulating that it was Ibn Qu, the crown prince, who was staging the attacks to pressure his tired and aged father to give up the throne.

Knights, or *Farimas* as they were known locally in the Mandinka language, were moving up and down in the town, trying to locate the perpetrators while ransacking houses and spot-checking passersby, looking for a scapegoat.

Samu dismounted his horse, sweating profusely, he said, "I have to tell you something, I have the crystal." I was flabbergasted, as I had already given up on finding the crystal. "How, where, when?" I asked.

"Well, I pretended to be a complete drunk on the night of the fertility rites in Kukiya. I then made my way to the queen's quarters, where I used an invisibility-cloak spell which worked partially. I found her vault where all her ornaments were." Samu said.

"Wow, that's impressive, Samu. Got to commend you for that. Weren't the queen's guards there?"

"They were, but the partial cloaking might have appeared to them like a spectre, which scared them off. Furthermore, I don't think the queen knows what the crystal is capable of. She likely thinks it's just a gem."

"So, what are you going to do now?"

"We need to create some kind of distraction, so we can make our way to the Bandiagara Escarpment," said Samu. He knelt on the ground, opened his body bag —made with elephant hide—and began to prepare an alchemical smoke bomb. A bluish smoke suddenly erupted from the concoction he made, which alerted the *farimas* —knights—. Under the ensuing commotion, we skipped the queue and entered the town, and Samu headed in the direction of his old house.

Meanwhile, in the twilight lighting of the smoggy evening, amid the yet unsettled disquietude, a chilling silence arose, the background noise deadened at an instance, time itself became analogous to a drop of water sliding off slowly on a fern —when I saw Maya, my Hebrew teacher and friend being forced on a horse by a *farima*, her beautiful face churned up in anguish, and her clothes soiled, while she cried, trying to resist. The futility of her efforts was heart-wrenching, which filled me with rage, and I charged toward the *farimas* as they stood in guard.

It was a skirmish that ended with me face down on the ground and a few bruises. I could hear Maya screaming my name while the horse she was mounted on neighed and galloped in the distance, accompanied by barbaric invectives hurled at me by the *farimas* and commands to stay down.

***

Days later, Samu and I arrived at Bandiagra; still numb after Maya's brutal kidnapping, I vouched to find her and get her home safely. The Bandiagara Escarpment was a mysterious place, a plateau with a diverse vegetation and a multiplicity of medicinal herbs. Oases of intense greenery dotted the otherwise sparsely forested undulating savanna like the patterns of a cheetah.

50

The Escarpment itself; a sandstone cliff with dwellings made up of baked clay, built in the cleft by the Tellem people. They greeted us warmly upon arrival but appeared forlorn and lamented that they were being reviled and driven out of their home by the Dogon who arrived recently. Indeed the Dogon had outnumbered the Tellem, who were pygmies and had no fighting chance against the boisterous Dogon.

"Where is the Chief Suskup?" asked Samu, and the villagers directed us to the chief's house on the cliff. Climbing the cliff through rickety arrangements of wooden bridges was an uphill task but rewarding. We found Chief Suskup very busy sorting out manuscripts in his elaborately decorated tiny house, full of herbs —in ceramic pots— and terracotta figurines.

"Welcome, welcome, Samu, my old friend. We are living in troubling times," said Chief Suskup, a light reddish coloured pygmy with a bulbous nose and a gregarious but assertive disposition.

"Sorry to hear that, Suskup. With me here is Perig. He travelled all the way from Britain in search of the 'tool' of the Huskahs so that he can become king of Britain—" Samu didn't finish his sentence when I interrupted him.

"No... No, errr Suskup, you mind if I call you Suskup? So I never told Samu it's to be the king of Britain. I need the 'tool' —whatever it is— to rescue my friend who has been kidnapped by the farimas."

"Haha, I like this boy. He is changing the reason for his quest as we go along. Well, you can count on me to help," said Samu.

"I know, Samu," I replied.

"And you all can count on me too, but I don't know anything about the Huskahs. How can I help?" Suskup enquired of us.

"I have here with me a part of the crystal. Legend says a huge crystal fell from the sky and has peculiar properties which can help with teleportation," Samu said as he unwrapped the crystal from his elephant hide bag. The crystal was about the size of a clenched fist and had a violet appearance.

"You fool Samu...What have you...?" Chief Suskup stammered angrily. "Are you trying to kill yourself? Where did you find this?"

"I found it in the vault of Queen Mi-nana at Ku—" Samu tried to explain, looking confused by Chief Suskup's reaction.

"Remove your robe now. The crystal drains human life force. It must not be carried like that," Chief Suskup exploded, interrupting Samu but trying to contain his anger.

Samu removed his robe and on his back was a huge patch of a symmetrically distributed skin lesion. "Count yourself lucky to still be alive, my friend," the chief said, who seemed to have finally calmed down after examining Samu's benign abrasion, his words resounding as he led us toward the back of his house, which opened up into a cavern.

"For hundreds of years, my people used these tunnels to escape attacks from human traffickers and now from Muhammadans. These tunnels are too small for the Dogon or outsiders to use, and that is how many of the Tellem fled the recent Dogon encroachments. The ones that remained have taken wives among the Dogons. There are some tunnels that you and Perig can fit, though. This way, watch your heads."

***

We squeezed through several tunnels led by Chief Suskup. "The Dogon are very studious people, so they will learn a lot from the Tellem priests who decide to stay behind," he continued.

"Are you remaining here?" I asked.

"Yes, I am the keeper of these secrets, so I cannot leave. This is my home. When my time to leave this world comes, I will seal this chamber forever."

We emerged from the rocky womb of the mountain into an illuminated cave with sunny rays. "How is the cave bright deep in the rock?" I asked.

"This cave, including the tunnels, were not constructed by us, Tellem. Our ancestors found the cave and the tunnels here. They were built by the Toloy, an ancient race who found the cave a sanctuary from what they fled. The last of them died thirty-three years ago. Holes were bored through the rock from here to the top and affixed with bright crystals that channel the light of the sun. That is why it is bright— to answer your question," Suskup replied and looked around the cave keenly.

"So it must be quite dark at night, then?" I threw the chief another question, but this time it was Samu that responded. "Well, looking around, I can see right here in the wall, the *lapis-lunaris,* which like the moon, absorbs light from the sun, and there are also diamonds and other gems here that give a mild glow under pressure," Samu said, characteristically knitting his eyebrows in thought.

"You are absolutely right, and what's more, the Toloy had very large eyes specialised for navigating in the dark. This was their inhumation chamber." The chief said and pointed around at capsules in which the Toloy were buried inside.

"So, what's the extent of the tunnels?" I asked.

"It is said that the tunnels go all the way to Makuria. I don't think so, though, but they certainly go as far Kukiya, that far I have ventured in my younger days," Chief Suskup replied, "the Toloy taught us about astronomy, medicine, horticulture, animal husbandry, and even flying contraptions but they themselves only ate this plant and a few insects." he continued, pointing at a cave-dwelling nettle.

At the centre of the cave were metallic spheres representing stars and other globes linked together by a thin metal and moved through gears—a mechanical ephemeris. Samu was at a corner, knelt down and looking at a manuscript, "I think I know how the crystal works," he said.

"Zounds!" Said the chief.

"They must be used together with other crystals to mitigate the harmful effects of the crystal—which came from outer space—. I think it has unnaturally high piezoelectric properties..." Samu looked at us momentarily and continued, "...the Toloy were using it for teleportation to distant worlds."

"This is their calendar," Chief Suskup said while pulling out a rolled-up scroll from a ceramic cylinder.

"If brain size is an indicator of specieal intelligence, then these Toloy must have been aeons ahead of us," said Samu while engaged in an act of sacrilege after opening an inhumation capsule to reveal a well preserved Toloy female that had died over three centuries earlier.

"Careful, please, careful with her. We must put her back properly," cautioned Chief Suskup, looking at the mummy with a reverential gaze.

Chapter 6: 'Thanksgiving' or Praise: The Toloy Calendar

The streets were narrow, though graced with impressive cobblestones, houses terraced, some even seven stories high with desert sands piling as residue atop rooftops, and a chaotic but pleasant atmosphere. The pathways were shaded by multiple coloured textiles spread across from one end to another, creating a colourful ambience. However, only a small quarter of the once large and impressive city of Al Fustat remained after a state inflicted fire ravaged the city as a defensive measure against attacks from the Kingdom of Jerusalem.

It had been over a year since I was at Bandiagara Escarpment. Samu still had not figured out how the crystal worked or how to use it safely and had since returned to Timbuktu working tirelessly and fervently. Search as I did, there was not a single trace of Maya, who had been kidnapped by the *farimas*. Following a slave trail, I arrived in Mizraim, at the city of Al Fustat, which was in a dismal state.

I recalled the night of the fertility rites at Kukiya. The titles given to the different groups, the 'Children of *Usetorohila*' for instance, is none other than the children of Uset or Isis, Ra, and El or the Children of Israel. *"What then makes people refer to the queen of Kukiya and her people as pagans?"* I wondered.

Chief Suskup explained in the last dry season that the Toloy calendar marks points in time or predicts times when people will emerge with a misconstrued idea of a particular custom, which will spread far and wide. He further said that the Toloy calendar was the oldest and most accurate calendar in the world.

"Good afternoon, Ma'am," I said, greeting an elderly woman who was a curator at the Synagogue of Western — Tunisian— Y*ews*.

"Do not greet her! She is a grimalkin," yelled a grumpy old man.

"You would know, you are my husband, and what are you?" she replied. I made my way into the synagogue in a thriving ethnic Hebrew quarter of the city.

"I was hoping maybe someone can help me understand this calendar," I said and then removed the Toloy calendar from its ceramic encasing.

"Let me take a look," replied the old curator, who was now joined by her middle-aged son and husband. "I have never seen anything like this," she continued, "but you've certainly come to the right place."

"Psss! Pass me the candle. I can't see properly," she asked her son as the darkness of night crept. "These look like markings of the stars. Where did you find this?" she asked.

"I found it in a village far in the west of Bilad Asudan across the great desert," I replied, hoping she would not have too many questions. She looked content with the answer and carried on scanning the scroll.

Over four hours later, and after consultations with their learned, she motioned for me to approach her. "Have you finally deciphered it?" I asked.

"Yes, once you get the hang of it, it's not too difficult," she said, pointing at the upper left corner of the scroll and explaining further. "Ahh, the Toloy, as you call them, believe that 'Eu-Petah' has four sons, rotating around him."

"What is Eu-Petah?"

"In their language, they call it *Dunna Tolo Unuum*, but over here, we know it as Eu-Petah, which is a god in the sky, a power," she said, seeming very excited about the Toloy calendar.

"How do you know they call it that in their language?"

"I consulted Rabbi Oleysh, and he read it from an old book at the library." She replied.

"It's fascinating that the Toloy have been documented," I commented, to which the old curator nodded in agreement, "They talk about a star called *shira* or sirius and that it has

59

two companions and that one is four times lighter in weight than the other and moves at a larger and circular orbit. The Toloy believe that they came from *Shiga Tolo* or sirius, and they further distinguish between the heavenly bodies such that; non-moving stars are called *Tolo,* like the sun, and the heavenly bodies that spin around another are called *Tolo Tanazze* and others that move around others, called *Tole Gonnoze,"* she said.

"Interesting, so they were some kind of astronomers, huh?" I threw another question, and the good-natured curator replied, "This is not just one calendar. This is a combination of at least seven calendars. I can identify a solar calendar, a lunisolar calendar, a lunar calendar, a calendar of venus, and a calendar of shira or sirius. I can't seem to identify the last two."

"Well, thanks for your time," I said, and the old lady replied, "Sure, please come anytime."

***

I made my way toward the door, but a voice called me back, "Hello, I'm Rabbi Oleyesh, and you are?"

"I'm Perig," I replied, "why are you called rabbi?" He led me to a tiny office on the first floor of the *yeshiva* overlooking the street.

"Well, I'm a rabbi of sorts. Where are you from?"

"I'm from the North. Sorry I've just never seen a rabbi so young."

"Aah, the word rabbi simply means master, a master of a particular law. In this case, I specialise in the laws of *Yuda,* though I am as yet just a student. I apologise. I couldn't help

61

you out more with your calendar," the rabbi said, swiftly standing up to extend his hand as a greeting.

"Oh, okay, interesting," I replied. By then, I was thinking about how hungry I was getting and how far I'll have to walk from the synagogue back to the city centre of Al Fustat, where I had been staying for the past three weeks since arriving in Mizraim.

"So, where did the laws of *Yuda* come from?" I asked.

"Hmm, inquisition, I like that. You see here in Mizraim, we use Julian Calendar and *Eakupta* Calendar," said the rabbi, who then wiped his tabletop and continued speaking, "in Julian Calendar, this is the year 1309, and today is October the twenty-eighth. You see there is no perfect calendar my friend, even the Toloy Calendar will have some intercalary days," the rabbi explained while stroking his short beard. He certainly was not as impressed with the Toloy Calendar.

"So, where did the laws of *Yuda* come from?"

"Mmm, right, it comes from the writings of Rabbi Rashi of Champagne, France," Rabbi Oleysh replied.

"So prior to him, there was no such law?" I asked.

"Well, I wouldn't say no such law, you know, these are customs, not laws in the real sense of what laws are. Real laws are unchangeable like laws of the movements of the sun and the moon— the kind of things for calendars, you know."

"I see, so calendars are the real laws. What exactly is a *Yew*, as they say?"

"*Yuda* means thanksgiving or praise, you know, mmm?" the rabbi asked a rhetorical question and then continued. "While a *Yew* is someone that gives praise or gives thanks to God."

"So it's not a nationality or a place, like from the 'Kingdom' of *Yuda*?"

"Yes, someone from the kingdom of God, the kingdom of giving thanks."

"Where did the Torah come from?"

"About three-hundred years ago or so, after the first crusade, the Hebrew community was in dire need of a creation of our own country, away from oppression, so we became united under our customs, united by a book, the Torah created by the efforts of Moses Maimonides," said the rabbi who seemed very lively following the last question.

"Basically, what you are saying is that Moses Maimonides put the customs together into a book called the Torah?"

"Yes, he studied right here in this *yeshiva*, right here in Al Fustat around 1168 AD, after his family was exiled mmm, *emet*."

"So what about Muhammadans? They are growing a lot now around the western parts, too," I asked.

"Muhammadans are like us. Some of them speak Hebrew." Muhammadans are named so because they give praise to God. That's what it means, you know h-m-d," said the rabbi, who then vocalised the root of the word — meaning praise.

"But I've seen them performing some rituals that you don't do," I asked another question.

"Haha, it's not some dogma. Anyone can perform whatever rituals they want. There is no difference between us, except for titles," the rabbi said with a smirk and shaking his head ever so slightly.

"Okay, what you are saying makes sense, but the people who call themselves *Yews* have certain rituals that they alone do, and so do Muhammadans," I challenged the rabbi further.

"Yews or Muhammadans, at the end of the day, we each are just trying to learn the Merkabah. All our scriptures are based on that. Even some so-called *Yews* do not perform the same rituals as other *Yews*," said Rabbi Oleysh.

"I have a friend who told me that before, but I've seen pagans in an ancient city in the Empire of Mali, going around a cube, and my friend said it's a Merkabah," I reasoned with the rabbi.

"Are they 'pagans' or just different?" Rabbi Oleysh asked a rhetorical question.

64

"So right now, this territory under the Mermeluks; are they Muhammadans?" I asked.

"No, the Mermeluks are Slavs, coming from the *Kaz-Kaz* or *Kaukasus*. They were captured as bondsmen, you know, bond-slav, not a free-slav, and forced to serve in the army. The women are mostly odalisques."

"Oh my, it's so sad," I said.

"Earlier on, the bondsmen around here were Turks, but now all the Mermeluks, including the Slavs, speak Turkish, and they are ruling this country of Mizraim," said rabbi Oleysh, who did not seem to sympathise with them at all.

"So basically, the Mermeluks are not Muhammadans?" I needed more clarification from the rabbi because he seemed to know what he was talking about.

"Yes, I told you, my friend, Muhammadans either speak Hebrew or Hismaic. Today the language is not called Hismaic anymore. It is called Arabic, which comes from the word '*mercorabia*' because it was taught in Hismaic so much that it became synonymous. Some people see that as a good sign that everyone will learn about the Merkabah..." the rabbi paused for effect, "...and a region where they teach it is called *merkorabia* and a person who teaches it is called an arabi/rabbi from the word *merkorabi*. That is why the famous Muhyī al-Dīn was called Al Arabi. He died only sixty-nine years ago.

"Oh, amazing information. I haven't heard of him, though, but I'm very interested in Muhammadinism or Torah knowledge of the Merkabah."

"Oh, I'm glad you are interested in 'giving praise'. Call it Muhammadanism, Kingdom of *Yuda* or Merkabah. We have tremendous material here in this *yeshiva,* and you'll learn a lot, mmm." The rabbi leaned back on his comfortable chair and looked around the shelves of his mini-book counter.

"So, I should be on my way, but before I depart, what exactly is the Merkabah teaching all about?"

"Well, you know these things cannot be divulged profanely. It will not benefit you now unless you study."

"Okay, I understand—"

"On second thoughts, can you unroll the Taloy Calendar again?" asked Rabbi Oleysh, his impenetrable eyes and inscrutable countenance suddenly giving way.

"Yes, sure," I replied.

"Aah, I see now," his eyes lit up as he looked at the calendar. "This is not just a calendar. It is arranged in much the same way as the symbol of the Merkabah. I did think it looked familiar," he took a deep breath and examined the scroll with his eyes moving very fast.

"What do you see?" I asked.

"They are marking days and months in which the heavenly properties are ripe for one to shift to another place, in which case the calendar is specific about the days of power. It's like the Night of *Proorizo* in the Hellenistic tongue," said Rabbi Oleysh.

"What is *Proorizo*?"

"The night of power, or predestination. An impressive calendar indeed. It marks all holy days when specific portals of blessings are opened based on the arrangements of the wandering stars and gods. The calendar is about Thanksgiving."

Chapter 7: Britain: March 1295 AD

"Get ready, Perig, will ya. Stop dawdling about; make a man of yourself. It's late in the morning already," said Aunt Monenna, who hurriedly passed me a mug of porridge and scurried off with a child in her arms.

"But I'm only ten years old. How can I be a man?" I replied, sitting on the floor while struggling to put my boots on.

"Oh, don't be a brat. You know your mother will be very livid with both of us," she yelled from the kitchen. Aunt Monnena was at least nine years younger than my mother and often took care of me along with her many children.

The rolling hills and fields were green as far as the eye could see, the air fresh and humid with early morning mist still present even as the morning advanced. The chirping of aves with the most beautiful of plumage and a tincture of floral notes, an attestation that nature herself made the isles an exemplar extraordinaire of her gifts. However, nature's beauty is beguiling and reticent.

"Stay still, dear Perig. Today is a big day for your father," said mother while we sat on a cold stone bench of an old Celtic Temple.

"Good morning, ladies and gentlemen, though our beloved *Yr Hen Ogledd* and the Kingdom of Gododdin has fallen, today is still a cause for celebration as our brothers to the south have defeated the brutish English in the Battle of Maes Moydog. With that, I say may the Huskahs drive the Jutes out of the Isle of Wight," said uncle, addressing a small crowd of family and friends gathered to celebrate. Father was seated near him but hardly said or did much, except for the occasional smirks and claps. The gathering at the ruins of a Celtic hilltop temple adjacent to our house lasted all afternoon before crowds began to disperse.

"Come, son, it's time for your sword training," said father, late in the afternoon.

"Mom said it's a big day for you today," I replied, looking for a way out of sword training and pony riding.

"No, I was just looking forward to it because I want to meet friends and family. I don't make a big deal of these battles," responded father, who was a stern man that had been part of the *Fyrd-Foereld*—a type of compulsory Anglo-Saxon infantry— though always dreamt of retiring as a professional sculptor.

"Sorry to interrupt you and your son, sir, but you must come, anon!" Aunt Monnena came rushing out to the courtyard of the house to announce the arrival of an elder druid.

"Yoiks!" said the druid elder who had just arrived, "look at this boy. He has grown a lot since the last time me laid me eyes on him. He was but in swaddling clothes in the crèche."

"Go say hello. The druid wants to see you, son," said father and I walked toward the visitor.

"Allow me to introduce myself, young man," the druid said, who was not more than my height at the time.

"I am Drestoloy Frett of Dunnicaer master-builder of Dunnottar, earthmover, mound builder, megalith erector and magician of the highest order, at your service, my boy, ehee," said the druid in a whimsical and quirky manner with a tonal rhythm. The druid had a large head nearly twice the size of an adult's, a broad smile, a pixie nose, long flowing curly hair and a dark brownish complexion, and donned an elaborately coloured long robe.

"Oh boy, what are you looking at? Never seen a Pict before?" he joked and continued, "give me your hand, let's see," he instructed. "Aah, lots of travelling to be done, my boy," said the druid as he performed chiromancy or palm reading.

"What more do you see? Please speak," said mother, worried as ever.

"This boy Perig will rediscover phenomena gone by, but he must be steadfast or make it, he will not. I see ruinous forces in the midst," the druid warned, making mother even more worried.

"Okay, that's enough, Drestoloy," said father, who never subscribed to divinations.

70

"Hush! Oh, son of Gruffudd, I am a Pict. I don't take orders from you. For me, only the lady of the house do I listen to," replied the druid, who came from a matrilineal society distinguished from the Wotādīni or the people of Gododdin, who have adopted English ways after being conquered.

"I see more," the druid continued, "the boy will meet a friend who will be of great help to him, and he will also be reunited with a kith from a time before," the druid said.

"Thank you for your reading Drestoloy," said mother.

"The pleasure is mine, my dear, just keeping up with traditions. The boy is ten years old and must have a reading," replied the druid. He thanked mother and father and trotted off towards the door while singing and giggling.

Heeding the advice of the druid, I stood up immediately and followed him outside so that I could start my sword training but no sooner had I walked outside than the druid vanished without a trace.

***

Weeks later, father was upset after word spread that it was, in fact, the Welsh that had lost the Battle of Maes Moydog and not the English, but defended his brother for spreading rumours of victory because he too—his brother—, just wanted to meet family and friends.

"Papa, who is Madog?" I asked.

71

"He is a ruler from Wales—," replied father.

"I heard it before," I interjected.

"No, son, you are confusing it with the story Madog which is a folklore. The folklore is about a prince who travelled across the sea over one-hundred years ago to find a new land," replied father.

"Drestoloy said I will travel across the sea too," I spurted excitedly.

"Oh, don't make much of what that druid says. He said when I reached nineteen years, I would get lost, and they'd search everywhere for me and not find me, but I'm still here, ha! He can be silly at times," father said with a small laugh and then left the house with his tools heading to his workshop.

I raced to the courtyard and picked up my wooden sword to train, but the sweet aroma of the traditional *bara-brith* transported me to a world of imagination, though I did not have to imagine it for much longer as mother called out for me to have supper.

"It's delicious, mother," I said, salivating.

"I'm glad you like it, eat up," she replied.

"What are Huskahs mother? Uncle said, 'may they drive the' —" but mother interjected before I completed my sentence.

"He was talking about the Isle of Wight. There are men there, who are very skilled in archery; 'elves', but don't you worry your little head about that," she said.

"Why are the Angles and the Saxons light men?" I asked.

"Not light men, the correct way of saying that is fair-skinned. Not all of them are fair-skinned, some are like us, some of us are fair too, like your grandmother who passed away when you were very little," explained mother, always patient with me.

"So why are the Huskahs dark-skinned?" still confused, I asked again, finding it hard to grapple with the idea.

"Because they came from the land of darkness, the dark continent or the black lands. So many of them are very dark over there," mother replied.

"Why did they come here?" I continued questioning habitually.

"Oh son, they come from a large kingdom of fabled riches —gold. They must be looking for more riches. I suppose those on the Isle of Wight are miners, so probably not too glamorous," mother replied with a thorough explanation, enough to alleviate my curiosity, but her stories only enchanted me further, and I asked yet another question.

"Why do people there have such skins?" I asked.

73

"Must be the sun. It is the land of summer over there," she said with a smile on her face and a kind contemplative look as she gazed at me while I enjoyed my *bara-brith*.

It was then that mother sowed the seeds of adventure in me and not so much the words of the druid.

***

The next day started off uneventful and gloomy, the sky a chaotic mizzle, typical of the blustery month of March. Down across the valley, a stream ripples as barnacle geese make a crossing. From a distance came the enlivening sounds of laughter and jubilation accentuated by the characteristic 'cracking' sounds of drums— It was Drestoloy Frett the druid, who returned with a handful of his clan.

"The days of the Picts here have come to an end, so we've come to say goodbye," said the druid.

"Why are you leaving?" asked father.

"They are burning coal near our habitations, making the bairn and the aged sick. Even our dolmens are being desecrated."

"Oh, I didn't know that," father replied with a sigh.

"Many of our young have been stolen and put in courts of amusement," the druid blustered with a mild frown—appearing angry. "But *ch'mod,* if we don't like it here, the only other options are to grow up or leave. I think the former is not an option," he joked. His emotions were seemingly juxtaposed, never lingering on the negative.

"We are going to miss you all," said mother while rubbing the hair of a little Pict— a child who must have been recently weaned.

"This is my helpmate. Her name is Drusticc. She will recite a prayer for you," said the druid. His helpmate, slightly smaller than him, emerged from the small crowd, her body covered in roses atop her woollen dress, fastened by a decorative brooch and a golden neck torc. The drummers among the group readied themselves to start drumming while others started humming as Drusticc began to sing the prayer.

Meanwhile, the druid wrote the prayer down on the hide of an animal in a strange writing.

"What is he writing, mother?" I asked

"It's a type of rune," she replied, "they can open doors."

"Doors to where?"

"Doors to the Otherworld, my boy," said the druid, "doors to the land of laughter and fun and youthfulness, goddesses and goddesses and more goddesses, perpetual bliss, hahahee."

"Can I go there and come back home later?" I asked.

"Oh yes, we are there right now, but if you want to go there forever, there is nothing to come back and do here," he replied as the dancing and drumming continued.

"So I can't come back when I go there?"

"On the last night of a waning moon, listen carefully, my boy, just before sunset, and you will hear a sound, that is the sound of *Bag Noz*—a ship— that carries the dead to this land, if you know how, you can follow them to Annwn: The Otherworld."

"Enough! Enough," shouted father. "I knew I heard you telling this child even more nonsense."

"But it's just a story," mother replied softly.

"Quiet woman! You should have known better. What is to become of him if you fill his head with this? Do you want to make him a dreamer, a weakling?" Father went ballistic. Apoplectic with anger, he grabbed the druid by his shoulders.

"Alright, druid, work your magic. This boy cannot remember any of this."

"Gadzookers! Zoonters! Jitterbugger... Nothing I mentioned is taradiddle," surprised, the druid tried to find the exit, "alright everybody, time to absquatulate," he said, while fidgeting about.

"No, you don't. You are not going anywhere. You think you can come here and just say whatever you want? Drinking your happy potions?"

"They are not 'happy potions'. It's just fermented sugar— something you people haven't invented yet, heehhaa."

"Huh—? I know exactly where you are going, either to The Hebrides or to the Isle of Skye. You are not going anywhere called 'Otherworld', so quit lying!"

"Okay, okay, give the child this potion, and he will not remember woohhoohaheee!" the Druid said and laughed, rolling on the floor. The crowd of Picts then left jubilating as always until they disappeared in the direction of the shore and boarded their ships.

Chapter 8: Timbuktu

At the darkest hour of the night, I was awoken by the gleaming embrace of a waxing moon reflected on the pellucid waters of Lake Faguibine, not too far from Timbuktu. The lake bed was extremely fertile and home to a vast array of algae, but a pungent smell lingered in the air, with a subtle but pernicious mastery which made me noxious. I was floating on a canoe gently resting on the stolid lake, and out on the shore was Samu standing with a rope — made of reeds and fibres from papyrus plants— attached to the canoe.

"You are finally awake. You've been out for at least twenty-five minutes," he said.

"Well, pull me out. I don't have a paddle," I yelled while trying to steady myself, holding the edges of the canoe.

"Yeah, of course," replied Samu, and he began to pull very gently and slowly.

"Why are you so slow, Samu," I yelled again, eager to leave the lake due to a sudden drop in temperature and my painful realisation that I only had a shawl and a pair of trousers on.

"Thanks, Samu, oh my, oh my, it worked," I said while climbing out of the boat to the swampy lakeshore highly sedimented by rotten trees, deformed swamp birches, dried grass and reeds.

"Did you find any relevant information on who captured Maya?"

"No, I just saw a memory of my childhood."

"I brought you here because there is a highly inflammable gas seeping out from the bottom of this lake, which is intoxicating, but it can trigger alternate memories."

"Alternate memories?" I asked, confused by what Samu meant.

"What you experienced is not a memory at all but a reality that happened to your double. While it may not have happened to you, it is still relevant. That is why you saw it," explained Samu.

"But I haven't seen Maya," I said.

"There are many theories on how this works. Some in the school of psychology refer to it as 'false memory', whereby the subject may recall an event that never happened based on some trauma," Samu said while getting his horse ready. He then continued, "but I don't see it that way, I think all knowledge permeates every nook and cranny of space. It is the brain that recreates a familiar environment in order to access it. That is what your brain did. The vision is a recreation of your childhood, in order to understand the pertinent information, received onto an interface we call 'life like'—it is now up to you to connect the dots."

"Oh, ok, Samu," I replied, "*I think I get the general gist of what he is saying, I hope. I'm just going to keep quiet. Can't wait to get out of here,*" I thought to myself.

***

It was a time of changing landscapes, a time of the formation of kingdoms and the carving of new territories. It was an age of enlightenment, a time of literature, a revival of scholarship, science, medicine, and of knowledge buried with the Hellenes—Greeks—, and I was at the centre of it all, at the richest place in the world, and where the oldest and largest university in the world stood—the seat of the Empire, Timbuktu. All this while the greater parts of Europa wallowed in superstition, treachery, scorn, fear, totalitarian and draconian monarchies, but the irony of it all was that

Maya was captured by the farimas, the knights of this kingdom, and not of Europa.

The year was 1311, and it had been three years since Maya's abduction. I walked down the streets towards the banks of the River Niger, and I was awestruck by the clarity of the river there— being closer to the headwaters which emanate from ancient rocks with little silt deposits.

"Today, the king has brought us shame. The king has committed a shameful betrayal. Today the king abdicates. Today the king renounces his throne, oh what a shame, what a shame," sung a griot, part of a folk ensemble by the outskirts of the city.

"What is going on here?" I asked Samu.

"I don't know," he replied, "shall we head to the Royal Square?"

Upon arrival, I made my way to a guard and asked. "What is going on?"

"The king, Abubakri II, is stepping down. He is preparing to go across the great Ethiopian Sea toward the Maghreb Al Aqsa," the royal guard replied.

"The Maghreb?" I asked.

"The word Maghreb means west," said Samu.

"Is there any land over there? The waters are the most tumultuous I've ever seen," I said.

"Oh yes, lands exist even beyond, but in conditions not necessarily habitable," replied Samu.

There were hundreds of people around the royal square, all interested in what was going on. From every corner, languages familiar and some less familiar as the king's infantry made an entrance.

"What language is that, Samu?"

"That is Tuareg, I'm certain, but I can't be too sure if it's Tamasheq, Air Tamajaq, Tafaghist or any of the other varieties they have," said Samu with a laugh.

The Tuaregs held up banners in support of the king. Being from the northern parts of the Empire, they feared desertification and were therefore pouring out their support for the king's quest to find new land.

"Wait, wait, wait, is that their script? I've seen that somewhere before."

"Yes, it's written in that script, called Tifinagh, which is an abjad script. An abjad script only has consonants represen—"

"These are the runes of Drestoloy Frett!" I cried out excitedly, cutting Samu short. He scowled at me for a moment and then asked, "And who or what is Drestoloy Frett?"

"He is a Pict from my vision."

"Hmm, very good, Perig, very good indeed."

Moments later, the king emerged to bid the kingdom his final goodbye with about five dozen small boats on the River Niger.

"Is that all the boats they are going with?" I asked.

"Oh no, not at all. They are not going with these boats. These only serve the purpose of taking them to the ends of the river where it drains out. There is a tropical delta to the south, which lies in a rainy forest," explained Samu.

"You are absolutely correct, sir. I overheard both of you earlier, talking about the Tuareg language. The Tuareg have to be part of this adventure because, over the centuries, we have come to specialise in navigating the lands and seas," said a man with shifty eyes lined heavily with eyeliner and a pointy goatee.

"Oh yeah? Have you ever been to the south?" Samu asked the man looking at him suspiciously.

"Yes, I've been. It's not too far from here where this river reaches its ends," said the Tuareg.

"So where does the river meet another?" Samu queried the man.

"Ah, ah, it's in a city called Jaa, I think," the man responded.

"You speak the truth. There is a confluence at the city of Loko-ja where it meets the Chadda River," said Samu, finally relaxed.

"My name is Ghaly, by the way," he introduced himself.

"Great, nice to meet you," I replied.

"You know they are still recruiting men who are willing to go across to the new lands if you want to go," Ghaly suggested.

"No, we are not interested. They already have over 400,000 men and two-thousand ships. They will also likely stop by and take more men from the Awori people of Eko who are master craftsmen." Samu responded adamantly.

Before the king boarded, he was called back by a notable who announced the arrival of another king from the South—the Kingdom of Kanem-Bornu— by the name of Ibrahim I. The king made an unannounced entrance to warn Mansa Abubakri II of the perils of the journey and that he had seen in a dream the rise of the nations of the frigid zones against the wealth and peace of Bilad Asudan but the king still departed later that day.

***

"Samu, why were you being short with Ghaly?" I questioned Samu.

"He didn't seem too trustworthy."

"But he proved that he knew what he was talking about."

"I don't know. It seems like he is holding his cards very close to his chest."

With those words echoing in my ears, I paced toward the market square squeezing through a small crowd of people and found Ghaly standing by the corner, looking suspicious.

"Ghaly! Ghaly!" I called out, but when he saw me approaching, he sprang off and ran away. I chased him around the city block and finally caught him after he was driven into a cul de sac.

"Why were you running? I just wanted to talk," I asked.

"Because he is a thief, and he stole my bag without me even noticing it," said Samu, who apparently ran after me.

"Ok, please don't hurt me," he begged, "I'm not really a thief. I have no choice."

"Blatantly unrepentant at that, what audacity. We should hand you over to the farimas. I thought I smelled something foul-felonious about you," Samu sparked.

"Samu, don't chastise him too much. He said he had no choice. Alright, better speak up."

"My partner was captured. I searched and searched and finally met a man across the desert who knew something. Please, you've got to believe me," Ghaly asserted with a mild sob.

"He speaks the truth," said Samu.

"So the man is asking you for money?" I asked.

"Yes, gold, silver, pennies, or precious stones, crystals, anything."

"Has the man given you any indication that he knows where they took her?" I asked.

"It's a he."

***

Days later, we sat at Samu's house deciding how to follow Ghaly's lead with a sure proof stratagem or if we should even follow it, but it was the only promising lead we had had in years. It was the day that the deputy of the king made his first speech since the departure of the king. Samu's house was in an affluent and bourgeois quarter of the city, not too far from the royal square, situated in a row of houses shaded by copaiba balsam trees on either side, all the way to the royal square— creating a shady backdrop.

From the balcony of the house could be seen a Hebrew library which attracted my attention. As it was one of the only two regional languages that I spoke, I wanted to take a look, but there were more worrying matters at hand.

"I wish I could hear the king's speech," said Ghaly.

"I'm not interested," I replied to Ghaly, who was seated on the balcony looking far out at the royal square where the king gave a speech.

"The son of Kanku, as they call him, will do well when he becomes a Mansa if his brother does not return from across the sea. That's his mother's name Kanku, a remnant of the matriarchal origin of the Mandinka," said Samu.

"We Tuaregs are also matriarchal. To this day, property is inherited from the mother's side, well, some of us still are actually." Responded Ghaly.

"Alright, gentlemen, sorry to cut you off, but we have to get up and follow this lead," I said.

"Right," answered Ghaly in a hushed voice as though fearful.

"Why do you answer like that? Are you still afraid of that man?"

"A little bit."

"No need to fear. We will go at night just in case he has people looking out."

"Brilliant plan," said Samu.

"Did you see the people that kidnapped your partner?" I asked.

"Yes, they were dressed like farimas but…but…"

"But what? I can't believe you still have more information that you haven't shared all these days, but what?"

"But I knew they were not farimas."

"Why not?"

"They had an inner vest that had a peculiar crest."

"Can you illustrate?"

"Yes, let's go outside. I'll draw it on the ground."

"This is unbelievable. This is the same crest from the queen of Kukiya, I think. I didn't see it properly, but I know it's not the ones that the marabouts use."

Samu looked surprised and then said, "We shall follow the lead tonight."

That night we prepared horses and food and headed west, and more than two weeks later, we were at the western shores of Bilad Asudan.

Chapter 9: Maya in Grenada

"Good morning, sir. What are you doing lying in the dirt?" said a street cleaner, "there are baths and sleeping quarters you can go to, free of charge."

"Really?" Replied Ghaly

"Well, yes, this is Andalusia, haha," the street cleaner joked.

"I know where I am, stupid," responded Ghaly.

It was early in 1314 that I began to feel the blistering polar wind of Europa against the skin of my face, but as the momentum of the wind built and the gust turned into a tempest at sea, I became overwhelmed by an enduring saudade that I had suppressed for years. I missed home, I had a longing for good old Britain, but I was not going to give up after coming this far.

I turned around and looked at my old friend Samu who was still on the journey just for the adventure. He hated sedentary life and had received news that his wife of ailing health had passed away, so he was more than happy leaving Timbuktu. At the same time, I noticed that he had taken a liking for Ghaly over the course of four winters since we had known each other, though he still called him a thief every now and then.

"I told you to come and take a look, Ghaly. What happened?" I asked.

"Fatigue overcame me, and I napped on the bench," he replied, rubbing his eyes, trying to slap the slumber away.

"It's his first time this far north. I can tell from the way he is behaving, these unripe citruses appear to him as superlative manna as *zaqqum*—a hellish plant—appears to the denizens of hell after their sufferings in the boiling pits of pus," said a middle-aged woman who was taking care of the well-trimmed but semi-arid garden of a hilltop *alcazaba* or citadel at Guadix.

"What a bizarre comment to make," said Samu.

We began to ascend the hilly trek toward the citadel, and the woman yelled out, "They won't let you pass the first gate, you know." However, that warning fell on deaf ears but not without caution. We carried on for a few metres but began to see guards emerging.

"Where do you think you are going," asked a guard of the citadel in a raspy voice.

"We need to see someone in charge," all three of us said in unison.

"This is your last chance, or you will be forcefully removed for trespass."

"No, we won't," said Samu. He unstrapped his bag of alchemical concoctions while I drew my sword from its sheath.

"Halt! I am in charge," roared a man with peculiar rings.

"I received information that my friend is being held here against her will."

"No one is held here against their will. Drop your weapons, gentlemen and follow me." The man nonchalantly led us through the defensive walls. "And who is your friend," he asked.

"Her name is Maya," I replied.

"And another person also traced here. His name is Gethin. He was kidnapped and sold here. We tracked them all the way from the land of the Great king Mansa Musa," said Ghaly eagerly.

"Hmm, interesting. How strange," replied the man.

Moving through warm, magically ornate interiors standing aloof to the semi-arid exteriors, we finally arrived at a banquet hall with a fountain at its centre, from which incense emanated from burning wood chips soaked in oil extracted from the rare Aquilaria tree. It was an imposing structure.

At the corner of the room stood my Hebrew teacher Maya, whom I had grown to fancy over the short period of time that I had stayed in Mopti. She stood with an enigmatic smile, resting her eyes on me, dressed in a tunic that came to the floor with embellished embroidery which did not speak of bondage.

For a short period of time, I was overwhelmed with joy because what I had set out to do had been accomplished, but in an uncanny turn of events, Maya stormed out of the hall.

91

Perplexed, I tried to follow her, but I was restrained by two guards and the strange man who had brought us there.

Over a week would pass before Maya returned bearing gifts and with her—a young man.

"Sorry for the way I left the other day," said Maya and then squeezed me with an affectionate embrace while sobbing lightly.

"What happened, Maya? Were you kidnapped and forced to live here?" I was pressed to know, but she looked at me with a dismissive gesture.

"Why don't I tell you everything over lunch? Shall we?"

Over the course of the meal, set up on a roof terrace, Maya explained that her father had just passed away the week prior and that the news of his death coincided with our arrival and so she had to leave for the city for the funeral.

"So, who *are* you, Maya?" I asked, and she dropped her mug, her lips parted ever so slightly, but just before the words were vocalised, Ghaly barged into the room head over heels in an excited stupor with the young man that had returned together with Maya.

"Guys, this is Gethin, my best friend. It's been so long," said Ghaly.

"Pleased to meet you, Gethin," Samu and I responded.

"So Maya, I'm all ears," I said, but before she could respond, a voice interrupted with bursts of giggles. A familiar voice, which said "Maaaya, me lady! When did you return?" It was Drestoloy Frett.

"Drestoloy Frett!" I said.

"Have we met, Sir?" he replied.

"No, we haven't," I said; he nodded.

"Well, me lady, at your service," he said

"I called Drest here to tell you everything, he says it better than me, but you know what?..." She paused and inhaled deeply, "...I'm just going to tell you myself. My mother is the Queen of Kukiya. She descends from Madog ab Owain Gwynedd who was a prince of Gwynedd that left

93

Britain around 1170 and travelled across the seas to find new land, fleeing internecine violence."

"Isn't that folklore?" I replied, looking toward Samu, but he was far across the terrace, soaking up the sun in a state of meditation.

"The Welsh prince could not cross the Great Ethiopian Sea. Instead, he got lost near the shores of the northwestern extremities of the continent of Bilad Asudan. There, he and his men were rescued by a fishing fleet."

"So somehow, he ended up in Kukiya deep in the continent, and you came along?"

"That was one hundred and forty-four years ago, Perig," replied Maya mockingly, "I haven't been here that long. I'm only human, you know," she quipped.

"She is a very beautiful woman, hasn't changed much, her dimples still appear when she smiles, her hair still thick, wrapped up in a bun, her brown eyes bedazzling, her lips rich and full of colour, her hands dainty, her eyes still holding the flames of passion, her slim athletic build still alluring...but beyond that, she wraps her arms around the soul of the world, she stands with humanitarian causes, she is a leader. She touched me with her love and tenderness, and I appreciate the Hebrew lessons but why didn't she look for me, why was it I that looked for her?" I must have

appeared pensive, lost in thought when she spoke, "Are you even listening?"

"Yeah, who kidnapped you?"

"My late father ordered it"

"And your mother?"

"She hid it from us, that we could live here in Guadix."

"So you are *someone* now?"

"I am in a better position to help people or do whatever I want," responded Maya.

"And what about you? How did you end up here?" I addressed Drestoloy Frett.

"My people fled the Isles of Britain a long time ago, the hands of destiny lead us to find the Welsh prince Madog living in Kukiya, married to royalty and unable to return home we settled with him, from whom generations later came Maya whose mother married the brother of the King of Guadix," Drestoloy Frett said while a young servant poured him some tea.

"So Maya is some kind of Baroness?"

"No, I am a viscountess in my own right."

***

Before the light of day dimmed and merged with the blackness of night, Maya and I ventured to the east side of the fortress. In our stroll, I could see from a vantage point the whole of the city of Guadix, which was spread out but also had clusters of housing closely knit, painting a quaint picture.

The citadel itself was composed of an entire community of people —from Bilad Asudan—working together as its nourishment along with their children, but among them, like an oddity, stood one child who bore the likeness of the Visigoths. I tried to speak with him, but he was shy and disappeared among his peers.

"Maya, who is that child," I asked.

"He is my child." Said a man who also appeared to be strolling around the fortified corridors of the *alcazabar* or citadel.

"Good evening, your majesty," said Maya and I followed suit.

"Oh, lose the title already," said the man.

Later that evening, the king invited us to his royal banquet, and while we dined with the finest food I had ever had in my entire life, the king introduced himself.

"My name is Abu al-Juyush Nasr ibn Muhammad, I used to be known as Nasr of Grenada, but now I settle for the title King of Guadix," said the king. He had a friendly composure, a deep voice and an eye for detail. He was young, about my age.

"Great to meet you, your majesty," I replied. The king was a visionary. He spoke of ideas of world peace and friendship among all nations of man. He seemed to be removed from mundane politics. I could see why he was letting Maya stay at the citadel, though I also suspected there could be other reasons, given that the king was no more than my age at the time.

"Your highness, are you related to Maya's father," I asked.

"Oh yes, yes, 'ayyah' Maya's father was my stepbrother, a very dear and exciting individual. We travelled together to the cities of Bilad Asudan, to beyond the Hindu Kush, and to a land far and wide in Al Murak— the lands of the Anasazi across the Ethiopian Sea, and to the lands of Sin; in the East."

"You had your share of travel, your highness."

"Yes, Yes, but now I fear, I fear the end has come not only of my life but also for the Empire of the Maure or Sea." Said the king with a hint of distress. He removed his turban to scratch his head, revealing a head full of hair.

"Why do you see an end, your highness?" I asked, knowing full well he did not really mean 'lose the title' when he said it.

"We had problems with Aragon, Castile and the Maranid Sultanate from the beginning of my reign, my brother in law

97

is too short-tempered and myopic. They are using the old mentality."

"The Maranids are from the south, are they not?" I asked.

"Yes, but all skin folk aren't necessarily kinfolk. They are Berbers and bitter."

"Oh wow," I exclaimed.

"Indeed, ditto to that. Now the court is accusing me of loving Catholics, but James II of Aragon is a sensible man. The people here, the descendants of the romanised Visigoths, are no longer the barbarians that they were when we first came here under Jabir Al Tarik in 711 AD. That was over 600 years ago, and our resources are too stretched, but they— my people— don't want to listen to any talk about concessions. They will lose. That is why I abdicated."

"With all due respect, King of Guadix, but what about Yusuf's mother? She's a Castilian Catholic," asked Maya, a little apprehensive.

"I did not marry her. Though she is dear to me, her status here is that of a concubine. And all the other kings have concubines too, and not only from among the Castilians — who are relatively civilised— but even the far frigid nations of Circassia, and the kingdom of Kievan Rus, who have been displaced by the Mongols, some of them come here to live with us," said the king, trying to defend his position.

"But why do you need to take the women as concubines?" Maya pressed on with another question.

"So shall we just leave them to fend for themselves in the cold, outside, at the mercy of the people of Aragon and Castile? You see though the people have become slightly civilised, the Catholics are still not couth. While we bathe and shower every day, they are against washing, and they dislike reading. They don't have a single library. We have over seventy. We brought them civilisation, a torch to their dark, frigid world. We gave them books of science, medicine, and all manner of philosophies that we translated from the language of the Hellas and Eakupta. Look at the twenty thousand looms of Seville. Look at architecture. We built all the cathedrals." The king said with a sigh. He seemed upset.

I turned toward Maya, and she was ready to make a comment. Still fixating on the matter of the 'concubines', fearing the king might take offence, I asked a question to break the tension. "So, your majesty, why is this called the Maure or Moorish Empire? Do you think it should be referred to by another name?"

"Hmm, yes, it would certainly be more befitting to call it the Empire of *Nur*—light— because we are spreading enlightenment."

"Brilliant idea, your majesty."

"Maya!" the king said with teary eyes, "and for your information, my darling mother Shams al-Duha was a Castilian Catholic and a former slave."

"Oh, I didn't know that, oh my, so that is why they accuse you of loving Catholics," she replied.

"No wonder Prince Yusuf, your son looks very much like a Castilian," I muttered.

"Yes, of course," he replied.

"So, how do you remain so dark?"

"The sun," he pointed to the sky and smiled. "Speaking of the sun, I studied astronomy as a child, and this is a starry night, perfect for observations. I shall retire to my observatory."

"Have a good evening, your majesty," we responded, bidding the king goodnight.

Chapter 10: Toledo: The Inquisition of Samu

Tensions arose, and crowds were chaperoned. The sun at its zenith, its rays reanimating timber-framed red-tiled roofs of dilapidated dwellings. The streets convoluted, a clutter of minds chatter, here and there a squabble, a scatter, a rattle, and rumours emanating from tittle-tattle. The powerful, the zealots, the defenders of the Son, the Father and the Holy Spirit, trying hard and impassioned to bring the Kingdom of Heaven to Earth, while the ordinary, the confused, the pious, the naive and the sympathetic gather in shock—an evildoer, a denier of Iesus had been caught.

"In this session, you will be formally accused. Also, we have your sequestered items in a safe place," said the prosecutor, a middle-aged man with a boyish look and a mischievous visage creating a crinkled nose whenever he spoke. "And now the notary shall read the accusations against you." The prosecutor then moved behind the counsel table toward a window, making way for the notary.

"You are hereby being accused of the crimes of heresy, sorcery, sodomy, extortionate usury, and conspiring with Templar Knights," the accuser roared, his nose flared in contempt. Samu gawked, staring at empty space while seated before the inquisitors.

"I did not deny—" Samu uttered, trying to defend himself.

"Silence! You are not permitted to speak," an inquisitor screamed at Samu.

"Thank you, notary, may the Lord and Saviour bless you," said the chief inquisitor," and as for you, defend yourself if you have something to say."

"Can he at least have a defence attorney?" I asked but only got the response of an angry face, and then moments later, the response came, "There cannot be a defence attorney, for now. It is time for God to judge him." Samu's face was transformed by awe.

"I have nothing to say," responded Samu.

"Did you commit the crimes?" The inquisitor asked.

"Well, not really, but you misunderstand my ways." Responded Samu.

It was two weeks prior when the office of the inquisitors gave a warning to Samu. Since arriving at Toledo, Samu had intended to earn some money before departing, and we had set up shop, where I provided sword training while Samu taught quadrivium as well as horticulture. The inquisitors sent a series of raids —carried out by the Church's errand boys— to intimidate us into closing the shop, but we ignored it all. The final warning came in the form of arson and then, finally, the arrest.

"Not really? You are hereby assigned a defence attorney. However, he must inform us if he finds you guilty while preparing your defence. In which case, he cannot proceed to defend you," said the chief inquisitor.

The building stood in a collection of ruins —from the days of the Roman Empire—on the outskirts of Toledo, far away from public scrutiny. Samu sat at the centre of a poorly illuminated room while I stood behind a metal barrier. "I don't need an attorney. I can defend myself," responded Samu.

"Very well then, Samu, you have three defences permitted by this inquisition, *Tachas, Testigos de Abano*, and *Recusacion.* If   you succeed in defending yourself, you are free to go. Otherwise, you will be punished." The inquisitor said while simpering and then continued, "because of your relationship with the Viscountess, your punishment will be limited to a pecuniary fine and public flogging." The inquisitor moved to the back of the room, and the defence attorney returned to see if Samu had changed his mind.

"Permit me to defend myself by showing you that nothing I did was a crime," Samu exclaimed, asking the defence attorney to make a request on his behalf.

"It is important to confess, Samu, the hour for defence has already passed. That is why they sent the alguacil mayor to arrest you."

"But…" Samu struggled to find his words.

"You have the option of *Tachas*, which involves showing that the witnesses have no veracity. That is your best option. Take it, and we will proceed to your defence."

"Can't I just show them that their entire understanding is baseless?"

"That is not part of the procedure of inquisitions. They have already reviewed your case based on the testimonies. If you accept Iesus and we work to show that there was malice in the testimonies, you'll walk out of here a free man with no fines." The defence attorney said firmly, while returning to a small room in the corner.

Shortly afterwards, as the sun began to descend, the inquisitors returned. "After some deliberations, we have decided to grant you your request. You are very lucky to have friends in high places. You have the floor."

It was a time when the romanised Visigoths ruled by the People of the Sea or Moors were increasingly determined to have self-governance, and even though in 1314, only Grenada remained with the 'invaders', there was nonetheless an anti-Moorish atmosphere in Castile. Many children were named 'Matamoros' or killers of Moors.

Samu stood up, looked around the room, and then began. "First of all, I am Samuel Medad Hakham. I am now sixty-one years of age and speak a number of languages, including Classical Latin and your language that is known as Vulgar Latin, spoken here. In addition, I speak the language of the Hellenes, the language of old Eakuptah, the Yehudit language, the ancient tongue of Ashur and the Hismaic language. I am saying this to tell you that I know about the scripture. I got the name Hakham as a title, given to me by people in Syria based on the fact that I explained the meaning of scripture by logic and reason— they are called Karaites." Samu made an introduction. He spoke softly but clearly, using hand gestures to help with his oration.

"Go on," said the chief inquisitor.

"First of all, the religion professed here in Iberia was not born here. The religion emanated from Eukuptah, which today, in 1314, is called Mizraim, Eakuptah or Misr. It is a religion that began with the people of Eukuptah. Furthermore, in case most of you are not aware, the earlier

106

believers did not believe Yeshua was a historical figure. They believed he was a spirit messenger that a pious person could invoke unto themselves. That belief is what led Arius of Eakuptah to proclaim that the Son was created by man and that it is the Father that had existed since time immemorial. Which ultimately led to the Council of Nicea in 325 AD," said Samu. He looked around the room, maintaining eye contact with the inquisitors who appeared interested in what he was saying. I took a deep sigh of relief.

"And how do you know that?" The chief inquisitor asked.

"What he is saying is blasphemous. He should be removed," another inquisitor from the panel cried out. His eyes glistened as they caught the last light of the sun and his forehead wrinkled with anger.

"No, we promised to hear him out," replied the chief inquisitor, motioning for Samu to carry on, but before Samu spoke, the third inquisitor stood up.

"It was Emperor Licinius and Constantine who legalised and standardised Catholicism. Of course, there were differences of belief at the time, and there still are, but it doesn't make those opposing beliefs correct. You are talking about Arianism. Your point exactly?"

"I was just trying to establish the fact that my standpoint is not baseless. I teach that the Holy Spirit is the saviour. I have never denied Iesus," responded Samu.

"Even though he is wrong, we shall let him speak!" The chief inquisitor thundered.

"So carrying on, there used to be believers of Iesus systems all around Bilad Asudan, from Eakupta to Makuria and Byzantium, who knew that Iesus was an angel-like spirit that visits the pious and gives them the message of God. If that was not a thing, none of those ecumenical councils would have existed. The word 'Catholic' simply means universal. The ecumenical councils were just trying to establish a universal religion. Furthermore, Catholicism did not start in Judea. It started in Eakuptah, where they modernised and altered the already existing divine triad, namely Ausar, Ra and Heru and sometimes the third being Auset."

"Ok, so you think Iesus did not live and walk on earth, ate food, called people to the right path and was born of a virgin?" asked the chief inquisitor.

"Before I answer that, please permit me to establish further that in the earlier days, there were schisms and disagreements between the Western Church and the Eastern Church that had to be wiped out by 'force of arms', and you know what they say history is written by the victors," Samu responded, standing strong as he addressed the inquisitors. Samu was a proud man at times who held strongly to his principles believing he was doing what he did to help. *"I would have just agreed with them and begged for pardon,"* I thought to myself.

"Go on then," said the inquisitors in unison.

"To answer your question, let me elucidate the fact that, in my travels, I have come across cultures who worship gods that were born of virgins, gods who also had twelve disciples and gods who performed all the miracles of Iesus and have all the attributes ascribed to Iesus— a great star foretold their birth or wise men and many of them gave proof of their divinity at an early age. Therefore, this is clear that Iesus is an allegorical myth and not a historical reality. Are you following me, gentlemen?" Samu asked, looking intently into the eyes of the inquisitors who appeared emotionless, unmoved and unconvinced.

"Carry on," the third inquisitor said.

"Most of these other gods that I have encountered in my travels were 'anointed with oil....' Samu paused, making air quotes with his fingers to emphasise the similarities, but the inquisitors did not seem to have caught on. He then continued, "...many of these gods died and were interred, only to be resurrected three days later. They were also called

'Messiahs', 'Son of God', 'Saviours', and they were returned to heaven like he was, as well as being part of a divine triad."

"You speak lies. How can we believe you? How dare you say our Lord and Saviour has another like unto Himself?" one of the inquisitors exclaimed, pointing his finger at Samu.

"I have visited these cultures far and wide. From here to the Hindu Kush, you will find these and like you, they are not iconoclasts, so they make images of their lords fashioned in the most beautiful sculptures, and they even have scriptures compiled in 'books' made with 'paper' which you as of yet do not. The only existing scriptures now in 1314 are Mythraic scrolls held in 'Pagan' temples at the outskirts of Rome." Samu responded.

"You are right about one thing, we do not have complete scrolls yet, our writings are on parchments, but different books do exist separately though not compiled. However, you are wrong about Mithras if you think that is similar to Iesus. Mithras was born of a rock, he emerged an adolescent from a rock, and it is just a continuation of the religion of the Persian Zarathushtra Spitama, ha!" the chief inquisitor roared with a laugh, followed by further laughs from the other two inquisitors.

"He emerged from a rock? That is very interesting," I thought to myself. I tried to wave at Samu to get his attention so that he could use the humour that had erupted as an

110

opportunity to placate the situation so that he may be able to leave scot-free, but he was wholly animated, his eyes all-knowing and unwavering but with a compassionate glint.

"Well notwithstanding, Mithras is still Iesus. He might have been born of a rock, as they say, but that is still a miraculous birth without parents. Furthermore, he was born after the darkest day of the year, similar to Iesus; that's the twenty-fifth of December. Also, keep in mind, to this day, you can find caves where Mithras was worshipped in Rome, but according to St. Justin Matyr, Iesus was also born in a cave, you see the similarities?" Samu responded strikingly.

"Couldn't the pagans have just copied that? How do you know theirs is older?" asked one of the inquisitors.

"If you look at Pauline religions, Yeshua is referred to as the rock. Furthermore, the Nicean Creed —that you practice here— as I established earlier comes from 'Eakuptah', which literally means 'the stead of the rock' where the Latins and the Hellenes took their word 'petra' — meaning rock— from. Moreover, in the cult of Mithras, the leader or pope was referred to as Pater Patrum, which means the father's father. Isn't Saint Peter a father of scripture or a founding father?" Samu asked a rhetorical question.

Enchanted by Samu's eloquence, the inquisitors became carried away as did I, that as the millions of stars poked through the black of the sky, so too did villagers

111

conglomerate around the perimeter of the old building poking through the windows with all ears.

"So what do you make of the crucifixion?" asked the chief inquisitor, whose face was partially illuminated by the light of a burning candle.

"Before men were put on crosses as gods, it was snakes," responded Samu. Excited, I made a comment to add to what Samu was saying. "Yes, growing up, I used to see depictions of crosses with snakes hung on them all over Britain. On old temples from before Catholicism." Unknown to me that I had shifted the attention of the inquisitors away from Samu to myself. They noticed that about me were dozens of villagers that had apparently been listening. This angered the inquisitors because the session was supposed to be private, and with that, Samu and I were rounded up and thrown into a dungeon. A blunt force trauma followed from a mace and my face went crashing down—lights out.

Chapter 11: The Lote Tree of Girba

One midsummer night, as I lay within the belly or *querencia* of the stony old dungeon, gazing at the sky, a distinctive smell with exuding brilliance saturated the otherwise rancid environs. The smell was like citrus with fruity accents and a hint of spice. I looked around the underground dungeon— that had openings at the centre of its vaulted ceilings—and all around were flowers abloom. The flowers grew on piles of earth gathered around corners and in the spacing between the blocks of the walls. I got up and walked out of my cell toward a hallway that led to other cells within the dreary unfortunate dank of the dungeon, but a melodious humming soon drew my mind away from the rancour, and my curiosity piqued to find its source.

"Perig, don't you want to leave this place?" The humming voice suddenly stopped and spoke. The voice was coming from a shadowy enclave from whence the aroma of the flowers grew even stronger.

"Who's there?" I asked, moving into the shadows, careful not to stumble.

"I am from the village above," said a young woman with a captivating appearance dressed in a mono-coloured dress typical of the villagers, but she smelt of perfumes.

"I would have thought the dungeon had turned into a house of perfumery. Do you work in a perfume shop?" I asked, trying hard to figure out where the strong aroma, now intoxicating, was coming from.

"Forget the perfume Perig. I like the smell of the flowers," she replied.

"How do you know my name?"

"Shhh, I came to warn you."

"Huh?"

"My name is Heba. Listen, your friend Samu is ill, he has been exposed to the crystal for too long, and he is only still alive because of his Huskah blood," she said with a high-pitched voice, slightly nasal.

"So, what are you warning me about?" I replied, observing her peculiar rhythmic dance, gently oscillating around, picking flowers and placing them in her hair.

"I will get you out of here if you want," she said, her sonorous voice rebounding off the surfaces of the walls and her accent foreign and unfamiliar.

"Well, you seem rather sanguine. How do you plan on removing the chains?" I replied, pointing at the long chains of the leg cuffs that anchored me to the walls of my cell.

"The other two inquisitors have already died from mishandling the crystal, and Samu is dying. No one can help him here. Come with me. I need someone big and strong and muscular like yourself to help me flee this city of the

114

accursed." She said, moving her fingernails in the dent between my pectorals and sliding up toward my neck until she grabbed my jaw and whispered, "Please, Perig."

"Where will we go?"

"Wherever, Perig."

"No, I have things to do and people I care about here."

"Who? The Viscountess of Guadix? The journey from here to her is like that between the rising and the setting of the sun. Yet she has not done anything for you. Why was it you that had to look for her?" The young woman said, her pupils not dilating despite the darkness of the dungeon.

"How do you know that?"

"You speak in your sleep, Perig. I was here last night," she replied.

"Ok, I'll leave with you, but only after I help Samu,"

"Shh...Shh, they are coming. I have to go. Samu can only be helped at Girba. Follow Dhanab al-Dajājah," she whispered under the sounds of thudding footsteps above the dungeon. My head began to whirl, and between the sound of her voice and the thudding above, a somniferous urge overcame me, and all was black.

I woke up late in the morning with a splitting headache and began to scour the ground to follow the footprints of the young woman that had visited the night before, but the wind had rearranged the sands. I looked at my leg cuffs, and they had been unbuckled.

I found Samu in an infirmary for peasants—not too far from the dungeon— where the two inquisitors died. *"The young woman Heba was right. Who is she?"* I thought. "Are you ok?" I asked Samu, who lay on a bed of hay, his legs elevated and his lips chapped from dehydration.

"I'm better than last week. I have some water now," he replied.

"Listen, someone told me you can be helped, but not here. At Girba"

"I am in no condition to go to Girba. Go and learn how and come back."

"She said, I should follow Dhanab al-Dajājah." I said, hoping Samu knew something about that, and thankfully, he did.

"She speaks of the Constellation of Cygnus. Please, you must depart now. Make your way now, but shall you see the woman again, do not tell her you are departing just yet." Samu said as he lay feebly on the bed. His eyes sparked excitedly due to the escapade now at hand but followed by a sorrowful streak, realising he was bedridden.

"Please take care of yourself, Samu."

"I'll be fine. Maya sent provisions, they should arrive soon, and she sent her greetings to you too," said Samu, but

I did not reply. *"Hmm, Maya has her life, and I have mine. Or should I go to her and see her before I leave for the Island of Girba? No, I won't,"* my internal monologue engaged in a heated debate while I bid Samu my goodbyes and left Toledo.

***

The sands of the shores of the island of Girba were white as snow, which could be seen from over a mile away, even at night. The land stretched under lagoons, which our ship could not pilot over, lest it ran aground. Farther inland was a brackish water swamp that was a sanctuary for migratory birds, which I had to swim and walk across before I reached dry land. In the swamp, I noticed dozens of ship carcases, some of which seemed to have been deliberately scuttled together.

"Hey, I'm looking for a place to sleep for the night," I asked a middle-aged man who was fetching water from a well. One of the only sources of freshwater on the island.

"There are no wild animals here. Find somewhere nice under a tree and sleep eeh," replied the man, who carried on merrily.

"What?" I asked.

"Welcome to the Kingdom of Ifriqiya," He responded with a facial expression showing apathy while raising his hands in a carefree manner.

"Ifriqiya. What does that mean?"

"How do I know? That's what they call this Kingdom of al-Lihyani: our King. Who is a foolish and powerless king. We are constantly being attacked from the west, and to top it all up now, we have pirates from the east."

"Sorry to hear that. Listen, I need to find the Hebrew quarter. I need some old scrolls," I asked the man.

"The Hebrew quarter is in the town of Hara Sageera and Hara Kebeera, but there is a man who can show you a place with old parchments, so you don't have to go to those towns— you need a horse, though."

I couldn't find a horse and had to walk for hours towards the directions I received from the man at the well. A few travellers were ahead of me, holding a torch. Hours later, I realised that we were moving in circles, and I decided to rest until daylight. As I prepared to sleep by the beach, I noticed the smell of the geranium flowers from the dungeon growing stronger and stronger, lulling me into a pleasant and insouciant state and sleep overcame me.

***

Early in the morning, I arrived at a valley where the ruins of a Roman temple stood, and I met a man and a woman. "Have you seen our daughter?" said the middle-aged woman with bushy hair and light green eyes with wrinkled corners. Her leathery skin tanned under the intensity of the sun, and her legs bowed with rickets or some similar ailment.

"No, I haven't seen her," I replied.

"Oh, but you must have. She often leads travellers here," said the man, possibly the woman's partner. He appeared a mixture between the Visigoths of the north and the Berbers of the south, with a big belly and a welcoming visage.

"Is Heba your daughter?" I asked, and they looked at each other confused and started speaking in tongues. They grabbed my hand and led me through to their dwelling full of herbs and the same flowers that I had seen growing at the dungeon in Toledo.

"Sit down, young man, please sit," said the man.

"She called, and you answered. We sent her, and she delivered, but who are you that hears a calling like that?" said the woman, who appeared confused, her head moving from side to side.

"Or rather WHAT is he that comes this far, for a friend?" said that man, whose eyes rolled around in wonderment while I sat there contemplating between screaming at them to explain what was going on or getting up and leaving the place.

"Ok, the two of you have lost me. I'm leaving," I said and stood up.

"Please wait, please, you can help us all," they said in unison.

"Explain then, now!" I yelled.

"Every night, we called out. Every night we performed rituals and sent notes into the belly of the earth for he who hears to hear," the man said as he sat on the stone slabs of the old Roman temple upon which their wooden abode was constructed.

"Please tell me about Heba. Please tell me about her. How did she speak, how did she look, was she older?" The woman went on and on, mumbling with grief.

"What happened to her?" I asked.

"She was killed by the hybrids three years ago. Our dear daughter," said the man.

"But…but… I saw her in Toledo," I replied.

"Mm-hmm, you are no ordinary man," the man responded.

"But how?"

"All minds are connected. Heba is our essence together, so when we send our intentions out to the universe, it materialises as our love, our loving daughter but unfortunately, sometimes in our imaginative affair, a longing feeling emerges which causes Heba to move in circles or to say the wrong things."

"*Hmm, that explains the will-o'-the-wisp on the way and also how she was oscillating at the dungeon,*" I thought to myself.

"Would you like some food?" asked the woman. I was hungry, but I rejected their offer.

"So why exactly did you lead me here?" I asked.

"So that you can help all of us, the world needs help," they replied in unison.

"How can I help, and what exactly are the flowers?" I asked. The woman stood up from where she was seated, her joints popping and creaking, and made her way to the chest upon which they placed cushions which they sat on. She opened the chest and brought out a book that had pages made from the cyprus papyrus plants that I encountered in the wetlands when I arrived on the island of Girba. The book was sewn together against the hide of a rhinoceros.

"Interesting book," I commented.

"Shh… They don't know we have this book. This is just the first chapter," said the man, carefully putting his hand on his partner's shoulder as she diligently turned the pages of the old book.

"This book is the Gospel of Gnosis, from which other books were copied. This book can rid humanity of the dark one, Yaldabaoth," said the woman, her wrinkled hands rubbing the pages with great reverence. She turned to a page that had a familiar crest that I had seen before with the marabouts at the Old Mosque in the city of Gao.

"What is that crest?" I asked.

"It is an ancient symbol. I don't know its origin," the man replied, squinting his eyes and rubbing his hairless chin.

"The flowers you asked about earlier…" said the woman, who gently plucked one,"…these flowers are from the tree called *Sidrat al-Muntaha.*"

"Hmm, it looks like the jujube fruit that Samu and I were offered at the Old Mosque. Hmm, what is going on here?" my mind paced, trying to connect the dots. "So, what do I do with all this information?" I finally asked.

"The hybrids have been driven away from here due to activities of pirates, but you must go to the mainland and find a fresh heart of a hybrid and return here. Hurry up. There is no longer any time."

Chapter 12: The Highland Hybrids

I travelled south farther into the Kingdom of Ifriqiya on the mainland, arriving at the fertile grasslands of Jifara. A farming community consisting of a few hamlets. There, I made inquiries about the Hybrids, but I was only met with blank stares. Nobody knew anything about the hybrids, so I had to stay to rest for a few days. It wasn't until after a week that I met someone who directed me farther west to a mountainous crossroads where two mountain ranges intersected. I finally arrived at a place that fit the descriptions that I had received. A large hole was quarried in the ground from which artificial caves were carved out to create dwellings, but still, I saw only humans.

"Are there any hybrids here?" I asked a teenager, but he could not understand my language of communication and so tried to communicate with sign language. He gestured by shaking his head in a manner that meant he did not know what I was talking about. Shortly after, another teenager emerged from the rocky dwellings and replied. "Do we look like troglodytes to you?"

"No, you absolutely don't," I replied.

"They don't live here anymore," she said.

That night while I lay on the ground near a small bonfire prepared by the people of the village— that I came to know as Matmata—, looking at the starry sky, I recalled the words of Heba, the apparition, who told me to follow Dhanab al-Dajājah. I also recalled Samu saying I should keep going south until the brightest one in the bird of Cygnus is just above the horizon in September. I did not know what all that meant, but I decided to count my losses and head south. I also began to ascend farther up the mountain range instead of travelling on the plains.

Early one morning, I arrived at steep-sided mesas which were either separated by huge valleys or narrow ravines on either side— a dangerous mountainous climb where my horse could not go any farther. It was an extremely arid region with limited vegetation, so I tied my horse by a dead tree stump where wild alfalfa shrubs grew, and he was very happy to take a rest and dine while I began the ascent.

"What are you doing this far out here?" a middle-aged man asked.

"I am looking for the Hybrids," I replied.

"The Hybrids are few now, and they hide very well, so you may not see them, but they love the rain, and it's raining today," said the man who was holding a dead rabbit, a few bags and a dagger.

"Are you a hide trader?" I asked.

"That's correct. You'll need to dull your smell; even I can smell you. It's like you haven't showered in days." said the hunter with a laugh.

"I left my horse down the valley. I would've used his urine," I replied.

"Take this dead rabbit and rub it all over your body. The hybrids have a powerful nose," the hunter said and headed on, making his descent.

Shortly after, just as the hunter said, I noticed the hybrids emerging from their caves playing in the rain. There were at least thirty-five hybrids that were out, and communicated with each other using a primitive form of speech, though I heard some familiar words being pronounced. I dropped my weapons, raised my hands and approached the hybrids, but they fled in fear, so I approached the caves. I picked up my weapons and headed into one of the openings, which had tunnels.

I could hear the hybrids screaming, hooting and pant-grunting, and finally, a tunnel opened up to a mountain summit where the hybrids did not run. Instead, they were looking at me keenly. I noticed some of them grouped themselves apart and appeared more human, less animal. That group of five communicated in an archaic form of the Tamazight dialect of Ifriqia.

"Can you speak?" I asked a young female who wasn't afraid to approach me.

"Speak, I yes," she replied, using an assortment of hand gestures. She was soon joined by two males.

"Only you speak?" I asked.

"No, papa speak," she replied, motioning for me to follow her. I followed her deep into the tunnels carved out at the side of the mountain, which could not have been built by them. "*The craftsmanship, though crude, was done by masters*," I thought to myself. Soon we arrived at a room which had furniture, probably stolen from a crashed caravan, including carpets and cups made from hollowed out calabashes—I was impressed. The hybrids then forced me to sit down by placing their hands on my shoulders and applying pressure, and they also surrounded me from every side and started grunting and hooting loudly, but whenever I moved, they would run away in fright.

Moments later, an older hybrid who looked almost human, made an entrance. "I am Papa," he said, his voice less high pitched and his body less hairy. He had massive and veiny wrists, short legs, and a very long and hairy back which merged with the hair on his head. His eyes nestled deeply in his skull, which created a permanent shadow — due to his heavy set of brow ridges—.

"I am Perig. Nice to meet you," I replied the older hybrid, who acknowledged it with a slight smile revealing his long canines, and I also noticed a fresh shaving scar on his neck. *"He must have been shaving when I arrived,"* I thought to myself.

127

"Why you come?" he asked, his large hazel coloured eyes sparkling and his eyebrows moving involuntarily. He then gave a loud short cry while gesticulating for the other hybrids to leave his room. At that moment, I could not tell him why I was there. The hybrids were human, or even if not human, they were animals of a very high order which I could not bring myself to slaughter.

"I am a friend," I replied. Looking around his room, I noticed the peculiar symbol that I had seen with the marabouts, the same symbol that was in the Book of Gnosis on the Island of Girba. "What is that?" I asked, pointing at the symbol, but his expression began to change. His eyebrows came down and closer together, his eyes glared, and the corners of his lips narrowed. For a split second, he seemed angry, and then he said, "this not good," while pointing at the symbol.

The hybrid elder then made a short whistling sound, and a very tall female entered the room, which she had to bend severely just to go through the opening. The smell inside the cave was acrid and the heat stifling, but a calm breeze came in, easing the atmosphere as the rain stopped. The female came bearing fruits that they had picked from the valley. She offered me, and I took two berries and kept them inside my bag, and in exchange, I offered her and the elder hybrid the fruits of the flower from the Island of Girba, which they accepted happily.

The female hybrid had long curly flowing hair all over her body, but as she sat and the hair moved, I noticed an infant suckling her breasts. *"These are magnificent creatures. They are kind too,"* I thought to myself. "I am leaving, thank you," I said, but the female scowled at me.

"Now night. Morning you go," said the female hybrid. She got up and motioned for me to follow her. I followed her down a dark tunnel, her child still clinging to her long brown hair. "You sleep here," she said and turned around.

"Wait, what is your name?" I asked

"Nene," she replied and left. I looked around the tiny room, which did not have a door, nor did it have a window. *"I would be out of my mind to sleep here,"* I thought. So I waited a short while until all the hybrids were fast asleep and began to walk toward the exit. Their snoring created a discordant sound, but they were very light sleepers, and before I reached the exit, many of them were already up and around the cave entrance, including the hybrid elder who was leading a ritualistic procession. The hybrids had created a wicker figure about the size of a human, made with shrubs and bones, placed at the centre of the cave entrance. I hid behind rock outcroppings watching, as a young hybrid was dragged from its mother while she resisted, shouted, barked, bit, and cried. The young hybrid was held down by four grown hybrids, each holding a limb, while the elder hybrid held an Oldowan tool and, with tremendous force, shattered open the chest of the young hybrid bringing his heart out. Blood splattered all over the elder hybrid's face. The hybrids then began to roar, grunt, whine and hoot.

The heart was placed on a makeshift altar near a collection of quartz crystals, and then the elder directed the subordinates to run inside the cave to retrieve something. Little did I know that they were looking for me. I looked on in awe but let out a loud cry as fangs sunk into my shoulders— the hybrids were attacking me. I pulled out my sword, ran toward the altar and grabbed the heart and took off.

***

The descent down the rocky, barren landscape was menacing, steep, and unfamiliar under the gloomy twilight of dawn, accentuated by the hot pursuit from the hybrids, but I made it down safely. The battle cries diminished the farther down I went until they stopped altogether. I arrived at the foothills where my horse was tied, but the horse was nowhere to be found. *"The hide hunter must have stolen my horse,"* I thought to myself while straining my eyes, peering into the dim lighting in the direction of the rising sun and headed toward the north east.

It would take the whole day before I arrived at the Island of Girba and another day before I reached the valley where the ruins of the old Roman temple were, but upon arriving, I noticed the dwellings of the man and woman who sent me to retrieve the heart of the hybrid had been destroyed and they — vanished without a trace. The whole place was ransacked and torched with all the hallmarks of a kidnapping, likely the activities of pirates or slavers. Luckily, within the charred furniture and the wooden frames of the house, I spotted the chest that the couple used as a seat. I quickly opened it, and surprisingly, the Book of Gnosis had not been burned. With

131

gratitude, I placed it in my bag and made my way toward the shores to find a place to retire.

Chapter 13: The Kohanim/Priests

The very next day, I found a nice shade in an oasis of eucalyptus trees where a natural spring flowed, providing fresh water for the villagers. There were a few girls playing by the spring while their cattle grazed the scanty grasslands farther afield. I opened the Book of Gnosis and glanced through the first page, which had pictures, but the book itself was written in a bygone language which I could not decipher. On the second page, I noticed a note written in Hebrew on a parchment that had been inserted between the pages, which read— *'It is Kahina and Igider, the parents of Heba. Hope this meets you well. If you have managed to secure the heart of a hybrid, then congratulations, you must now find the Huskahs— follow their crest. We had to leave during the night due to pirates. The woman you care about cares about you too, but her heart is with her work.'*

My mind raced back and forth, trying to understand what they meant and why they had to speak so vaguely. *"Aren't the Huskahs even a legend?"* I made my way to a small settlement called Hara Sagira, deep in the hinterland of the island and found a Hebrew quarter, where I hoped to find someone who could explain the book.

"You are welcome," said a woman who was sweeping the grounds of a small courtyard by the entrance of a community centre. "Thank you, please where can I find keepers of the laws of *Yuda?*" I asked. "Oh, you mean keepers of the *Halakha,* hmm, they will be located in the *kenis*—temple—. She replied.

"So, where is the temple?"

"Just right over there, the building with the walls around it," she said, pointing in the direction of the temple, which was small and looked like it had been built in a rush. I proceeded farther into the town by about a hundred feet and arrived at the temple. I was led on to meet one of the law keepers who was seated on a bench under a tree. "Hello, sir," I said, extending my hand to shake him. "You are welcome, welcome, welcome, please sit down," he replied. "Do you know anything about the Huskahs?" I asked, going straight to the point. "The what? No, I've never heard that word," he responded with a slight smirk, looking genuinely intrigued by my question. "Ok, can you understand any other languages?" I asked.

"No, I only speak Hebrew and the local language here," he answered.

"What do you know about the Merkabah?"

"Hmm, interesting question. It is a vehicle which can take you to realms," he said.

"Please tell me more."

"You see, sir, we Hebrews are a people that have suffered greatly. To cushion the minds of our children, we create

134

mythologies. For instance, the fact that there are no Levites on this island, we tell the children it's because of a curse from Ezra against the Levites which caused them all to die. We also tell children that one of the gates of the old temple was transported here and stored in this building, in this *kenis*—temple—. But you look like a man dedicated and with some form of urgency. What's more, Moses Maimonides, the compiler of the laws of *Yuda,* fulminated against the superstitiousness of the people of this island. Therefore, I will tell you what you need to know without any cloaks if I know, of course," he said, with sincerity. "Brilliant, please continue," I responded, and he cleared his throat.

"I know you have heard that some people break the word down to *mer*, *ka*, and *ba* and say it means light, body and soul, but I don't know about that. I know that in Hebrew, the word can be derived from its root meaning, which is, 'to ride'. Are you with me?" he paused and then continued "...something one can ride inside."

"By the way, I heard you are called Kohanim here?"

"Yes, we are called Kohanim, which means priests, but in the Arabic, it is means soothsayer or seer, you know *Kaahin*—a truth-sayer. So basically, the Merkabah is about repeating a series of phrases which will prepare one to visualise a light body around himself and journey into the seven heavens," he explained, stretched his back and then

135

continued, "I myself have never tried, and I'm not even interested. Many Kohanim speak of it but they can't really do it. Only the gifted can go to the seven heavens and meet God, only the gifted."

"So how does all this tie in with what Al Arabi was doing and his followers?" I asked.

"I am not too familiar with what he taught, but it is my opinion that it is from the same source, the arcanum arcanorum," he replied and then stood up and motioned for me to follow him, "come this way, let me show you this room," he lead me into the heart of the temple, and I saw other priests engaged in various activities, he opened a dusty jar containing a few scrolls which he unrolled. He pointed at the first scroll, which was placed atop the others and said, "this recounts the life of Akiva ben Yosef, who is believed to have journeyed using the Merkabah. Though he never made it to the seventh heaven. He was also executed by the Romans. It will be an interesting read for you." The priest attempted to move the scroll over to a table on the side, but he began to cough, so I called a young student to attend to him, and I opened the window of the dusty small room. It was clear that the room was not frequently visited.

"Sorry, why don't you rest," I said to the priest, who appeared ill following his inhalation of dust. "Oh, I'll be fine," he replied, moving over to a vase that had a lid on, which he unscrewed, bringing out three other scrolls. "This is *Hekhalot Rabbati*. It recounts the journey of Ba'al HaBaraita, also called Yishmael, who travelled to the higher heavens or palaces. He was very logical in his interpretation of the old laws of *Yuda*. Oh, and he was captured by the Romans at a young age. Another interesting read for you," said the priest. He further unrolled another script. "This is *Sepher Hekhalot*. It is also by Yishmael, about the journey of a man called Enoch using the Merkabah, which eventually transforms him into an angel called Metatron," said the priest who reached over to a shelf and picked up another scroll and made his way outside back to the courtyard where I had found him seated earlier. I followed him.

"So, what is that scroll you came out with?" I asked.

"This is the most exciting of the scrolls, in my opinion. This is called *Shi'ur Qomah*, literally the dimensions of the body of God and the mystical names of God. Basically, God is shaped like a man according to this work, haha," said the priest, who gave out a good laugh.

"So, how did it come to be?"

"Well, the angel Metatron supposedly revealed it to Rabbi Yishmael, but Moses Maimonides, the compiler of the laws of *Yuda:* the Torah, rejected it vehemently as a Byzantine forgery. You see, sir, that is why I stay clear from these scrolls. Hence why they are just there collecting dust.

There is no way of knowing if these men even existed or whether or not they had those fantastical experiences. Why are you so interested? Why don't you learn the law of governance instead or the science of irrigation? You are still very young and healthy," said the priest, shrugging his shoulders and moving his upward-facing palms from side to side, almost cynically.

"Let's just say I had some strange experiences in the past. I was led here by supernatural means," I replied.

"Ahh, tell me more," whispered the priest, rubbing his hands together.

"Ok, I had an experience years ago, where I floated out of my body, and more recently I met someone, a girl, but she was actually a mental projection sent to me by her parents," I voiced out, but I noticed a slight change in him. Crow's feet began to appear on the outer corners of his eyes, he leaned forward and gave out a huge laugh which alerted the other priests, and two of them came closer. "Ha! You expect me to believe that?" he said.

"We are here putting our noses on the grindstone, and you can do all that?" said another priest who had just arrived.

"I can't do it. It just happened to me," I replied.

"That's very interesting; very pleased to meet you, sir," said the priest.

"Let me show you a book I found. Actually, that's why I came here. I was hoping you could decipher it." I uttered and brought out the Book of Gnosis from my bag. The priests, now numbering twelve, surrounded me, salivating in awe at the sight of the book. I began to turn its pages while they looked on.

Finally, one of them spoke, "These are like some of the old scrolls that I have seen."

"What language is it, do you know?" I asked them, but none of them knew except one, an elderly man with shifty eyes and an uneasy composure, "It is likely Avestan," he said. At that moment, I realised that coming all the way there was probably not the brightest idea. I also sensed an uneasy feeling brewing, so I decided to leave.

"This book is just feculent trinket, just glamour," said the priest that I had been speaking with earlier.

"Why would you say something like that?" I asked, looking at the priests who numbered a dozen. "Well, you Kohanim have just been vapid. You laugh at one who seeks knowledge." I continued, my patience running thin.

"No, do not take it that way, young man, but the book is not valuable, sorry," the priest replied.

"I should go," I picked up the Book of Gnosis, securely placed it in my bag and made my way toward the exit. Just before I left the gates of the temple, I saw the young student

139

who I had called earlier to help the priest that was coughing, and he said, "Be careful."

***

I left the quarter of Hara Sagira and one day later arrived at the seaside town of Humt al Suk, where I found highly monastic Muhammadans who were more willing to help me understand the Book of Gnosis.

"I met some Kohanim, but they could not help me much with an ancient book that I have, supposedly written in Avestan," I expressed my reason for joining their afternoon conglomeration at the ruins of a Carthaginian villa by the seaside.

"The problem with the Kohanim is that they are very didactic. They say so many myths just to teach morality but lose the essence of the lesson," said a very fast-talking man by the name of Tahir.

"Take a look at the book," I said, handing it over to him.

After glancing through it very fast, he said, "There are aspects of this book that will take me days of study with the help of the jinn, but let me tell you about the Merkabah."

"Ok, please do."

"Find a cube-like the one over there, in the middle of the night, without any disturbance, move around it from this way. I can already see that your soul will experience it easily," he said, demonstrating the direction of movement to be employed. He continued, "my grandfather met Ibn Arabi. My whole family practice this form of Merkabah knowledge. Even if you don't see God, even if you don't travel anywhere, it will rid you of all sins and regrets that weigh heavy upon your soul."

"Ok, so this will ensure that I journey to a place where the Huskahs are?" I replied.

"The Huskahs, hmm, I heard about them when I was a child. Aren't they like from Eakuptah or something?" Tahir replied while waving at his young wife. He placed his hand on his chest as a way of thanking her for bringing refreshments to the male-only congregation.

"From Eakuptah? So they are real?" I rejoiced after finally receiving some direction on where I could find the Huskahs as directed by Kahina and Igider.

"I really don't know. Please have some sugarcane. It's very juicy all the way from Darfur," he said with a large smile while biting at the succulent perennial grass, which burst in his mouth while he slurped in the juice, creating a partial vacuum in his oral cavity, making his cheeks appear hollow.

"Darfur, where is that?"

"Land of the *Fur*! *Fur* means black. They used to be ruled by the brown-skinned Berber chiefs from here. So these Berbers gave them that name *fur,* but I digress."

"No, no, not one for sugarcanes. So how does the Merkabah tie in with Iesus?" I asked.

"Oh yes, as I was saying, move around the cube with an intense love for God and by God, I mean *wahdat ul wujud* —the unity of existence—. Be full of love for everything. Al Arabi was highly eloquent. He spoke in the Hismaic tongue so succinctly but at the same time poetic, symbolic and sublime."

Chapter 14: Unexpected Visitors

Early one evening, after taking a swim at sea and spending time sword training on the beach, I returned to my seaside room, where I had been staying with the Muhammadans, finding my room thrashed, my bags emptied, its contents flung and the Book of Gnosis missing. I immediately contacted Tahir, who informed me that masked assailants had broken in and had stolen the book. Tahir himself, as well as his students, tried to stop the assailants but were outnumbered and overpowered.

I stayed on the island of Girba and carried on with my studies after I received a letter from Samu saying that he was feeling much better and that he had stored the crystal away.

A month would pass, and the warm southerly summer winds would blow their dust before I felt the itch to take a night swim in the sea again. The moon was bright, and the clouds— tiny grey patches that seemed to go into infinity. The buoyant waves rested gently and glistened beautifully on the horizon, and the sounds of the sea— a rejuvenating serenade, but as I entered the water, I noticed a small vessel near the shore surrounded by boats and farther asea a ship with flags. I swam to the small vessel and discovered that soldiers from the western shores had laid siege on a vessel because of a treaty violation and that the passengers aboard the small vessel had to use canoes to get to shore. There were about thirty-five passengers on the beach, some of which were in very dire situations. I saw a man of diminutive stature trying to resuscitate someone, and I hurriedly went there to offer some help.

"Drestoloy! Drestoloy!" I yelled out.

"Oh Perig, help," Drestoloy Frett cried out. He was trying to resuscitate Gethin, Maya's brother.

"Breathe, breathe, you are okay, you are okay, you'll be fine," I said, after pumping his chest and blowing air into his mouth, which resuscitated him. A technique I learnt from my father the night he disappeared. It was a night that he had gone hunting in the King's land where hunting had been prohibited since the time of William the Bastard, who 'preserved the harts and boars and loved the stags as much, as if he were their father'. The tradition continued until the time of Edward I, when my father went hunting and vanished into thin air. That night, a search party was organised, but he was nowhere to be found. At least that was what we thought until mother mentioned a few years later that we had ran out of grazing lands due to the 'Forest Laws' which prohibited the use of King's lands, leading to monetary disputes with the neighbours, so he had to seek sanctuary at a church but which in turn required him to go into exile.

"Oh, I'm glad to see you, Perig," Gethin said feebly.

"Thanks for saving my brother, Perig," said Maya. I turned around and saw Maya standing there with Ghaly by her side.

"Our vessel got confiscated by the soldiers. Gethin couldn't swim when our overloaded canoe capsized. Thanks to Drest for bringing him to the beach," she said.

"It's great to see you all," I addressed them.

"Good to have all the crew here, ehh," said Drestoloy Frett, who had put on some weight over the months. I then led them to a guest house not too far from where I had been staying, and Maya asked to see the landlord to pay for the property. *"She must not be trying to leave,"* I thought to myself.

***

The very next day, I showed Maya around the market town of Humt al Suk, but I noticed a strange change in her, the way she looked at me had slightly changed, but I could not put my finger on what caused the change.

"So, how is work, Maya?"

"Oh, it's Sisyphean and too little time," replied Maya with a sigh.

"So why are you here?"

"Life in Guadix or in Grenada, in general, does not look so bright in the future to come," she replied.

"Why is that?" I asked.

"Some of the *Muwallids—mulattoes—,* you know those mixed people that work with us, they always talk about *reconquista,"* she replied.

"The *Muwallids?"* I asked.

"No, not them. I mean, whenever they go to the cities that have been reconquered by the Romance people, they always come back and talk about how hateful some of the Catholic people are, except for cities such as Toledo, which is more relaxed," She said.

"So you left everything behind just because of that and came here, to Girba, of all places?" I asked, looking at her suspiciously while shaking my head in bewilderment. "I plan to return to the Empire of Mali at some point. I just need to find a ship," she said.

"That's it? So why did you buy the guesthouse?"

"Because my brother is here too, and I don't want him to have to pay for rent," she responded.

"That's it, just that?"

"Yes, that's it, just that," she answered.

"So you feel like whatever you are building over there isn't going to last, huh? Well, that seems like a legitimate enough reason to leave. I know you as a visionary," I commented.

"Look, it's Drest, trying on a *jalabiya* over there at the market stall," she said, deliberately changing to the topic.

"Haha, he's funny," I replied as we walked over to him.

"You speak as if you know him. Just like you knew his name when you came to find me at Guadix," she said, glancing at me quickly.

"Good to see the both of you here," said Drestoloy Frett.

"You look nice," said Maya.

"I haven't pampered myself ever since my helpmate went to the Otherworld. I think I should start," lamented Drestoloy, his large brown eyes speedily scanning the textiles laid on the table.

"You were married, Drest?" asked Maya.

"Oh yes, my darling Drusticc was infirm after she lost a babe and passed away while lyin-in."

"Drusticc, huh? I remember that name from a vision I had. That's how I knew your name, too," I said.

"No beast of nature can affright me, but this that you said can cause shivers," he replied.

"Sorry to hear that," commented Maya while enjoying a *shakshuka* meal.

"You know that meal would be nicer with something I saw in Timbuktu called *tomatl*. They don't grow it there, but they bring it sometimes." I commented. They both looked confused, not knowing what fruit that was.

"So, tell me more about your late wife, Drest," asked Maya.

"She was very feminal that one, could never take the heat, but a big heart, she had. She would cook for the whole village," said Drestoloy Frett.

"Was she like you?" asked Maya.

"Yes, yes, she was also *abhac* like me. All Picts are small, like the Tellem of Mali. Initially, a people arrived from the Finn's lands who were similar to the Mongols in appearance, we lived in peace, but when the Norsemen arrived, even the brochs in which we lived could not protect us—They pillaged and murdered until we cried *fae de land*, *fae de land*,—from the land—."

"Goodness, that's terrible," said Maya.

"But what nation hasn't been conquered before. They drove us to the Shetlands, and from there, we went off to sea and arrived here and there," responded Drestoloy Frett.

"So, what does Pict mean?" I asked.

"Pict was a name given to us. It means rock. Can you imagine, rock, haha," said Drestoloy, his spirits rising as he burst out laughing.

However, in the midst of that pleasant conversation, a commotion arose in the marketplace, and the scene turned from a calm civility to philistine barbarity. There were looters while others were running for their lives, fleeing and screaming.

"What's going on here?" I asked a man who came running, heading toward the sea.

"I don't know. I just took off after seeing them running," he replied.

"What about the people stealing?" I asked.

"They are just opportunists but there are pirates in the market too!" The man responded. I looked at Maya and Drestoloy Frett and signalled to them that my curiosity would not let me stay there. "Wait, I'm coming with you," screamed Drestoloy Frett.

As Drestoloy Fret and I descended into the core of the market, I noticed some stalls had been abandoned while some merchants struggled to pack their goods. It was hard to believe that a few moments ago, the market blossomed with life only to turn unruly. At the square were three men, possibly pirates torturing a man who they asked to kneel on the ground. "Alright, that's enough. Let him go," I said.

"Mind your business," said one of the men, the tip of his sword by the chin of the man they were torturing, while the other two men drew out daggers. "If you don't let him go, you'll get hurt," I replied, pulling my sword out. "Standby, Drestoloy!"

"Oh no, I won't. I'm not afraid of these abydocomists!" he replied. The man with the sword rushed toward me and swung his sword, but I moved, and his sword missed me by inches. I used my elbow to strike his forehead, which made him stumble forward. Reeling from the hit, he swung blindly, which exposed him, so I used my foot to trip him, and he went crashing to the ground. "Stand down," I commanded, and the man agreed to surrender. Meanwhile, Drestoloy Frett had used a blowgun, and the other two men dropped their daggers.

"So speak," I said.

"We were not torturing him. He is a slaver," the three men said in unison.

"Is that correct?" I asked the man who was being tortured, but he stood up and ran away without responding.

"Hey, sorry for putting you on the ground. Next time talk when you are spoken to," I said, extending my arm to help him get to his feet. "Let's go after him. There is no time to explain," said the man. Both Drestoloy and I followed the three men into the town and toward the beach. We got on horses and headed south until we reached a shore where we found a ship and crossed over to the mainland of the

Kingdom Ifriqia, arriving at a small shipping town in the eastern extremities.

***

"So where did that man flee to?" asked Drestoloy Frett.

"They are slave traders, but that's not why we caught him. He has something very valuable—a creature," replied one of the men.

"A creature? Hmm", I commented.

We arrived at a port where dozens of people had been captured, mostly women from fallen kingdoms. "This is absolutely terrible," I said.

"Hey, we came for the creature. We are not going to take risks just to help free these *Saqaliba,*" said one of the men.

"*Sa*— what?" asked Drestoloy Frett while trying to use a turban to cover his face in order to blend in. "That's what they call the captured people— Slavic. Though these days, even the Romance People are called *Saqaliba* when captured," the man replied.

Many of the men among the captives were castrated, with a few who were captured to be enlisted in parts of military units. There were also women who were kept inside gullies with palm tree leaves for roofs. The women were only bound with ropes while the men were in cages.

"Have they been castrated here?" I asked one of the men while we walked around the port, searching for the creature. "No, most of them were castrated in *Praha* the ford or Prague. I have been there, a beautiful place indeed," the man's eyes blazed gleefully as he let out a cruel laughter.

"This man seems to be enjoying this. I'm sure he is involved with this somehow. Now it all makes sense... That's why the queen of Kukiya, Queen Mi-nana, Maya's mother, was rescuing the castrated Slavs and concubines. There's just so many of them," I thought to myself.

"Hey, what's with the softness? The situation has gotten better. Besides, some of the routes were founded by the Varangians—Vikings— who first began to sell the Slavs. So get a grip. It is what it is. One day they'll rise and make their own nations," said another of the three men.

"It's not right. Whoever started it doesn't matter. It must end." I said.

"Then you must take your crusade to the Radhanim who are working together with the Kohanim to transport captives to kings, especially concubines and eunuchs, but also men to work as soldiers. The Slavs are strong," the man responded.

"What!? Aren't the Kohanim supposed to be priests?" I asked. "There's usually more to it than meets the eye, boy," said the man.

"So, who are the Radhanim?"

152

"They are merchants, Perig. Their loyalty is just to the money. They travel all over the world. I came across them before. I think these men are right. Let's just free the slaves we can and leave," said Drestoloy Frett.

"That's not right, Drestoloy. I will free all the slaves."

"But Perig, since the time of Pope Zachary, over 500 years ago, there were slaves sold to the Moors of North Africa from Italia. They set it up themselves," cried Drestoloy Frett with a little apprehension. He wanted to leave unscathed, but I didn't care.

"I don't care!" I yelled, and with tremendous zeal, I began to break the ropes binding the wooden contraptions that the slaves were kept in, only to discover that some of them had their legs bound under lock and key. "Please help me free them, Drestoloy," I yelled.

"What fools! What about the Catholics? You think they don't enslave us?" One of the men yelled and ran in an opposite direction, farther into the port. "Yes, what about *Concordia discordantium canonum?* I've been to Rome. They have laws to enslave all Moors too!" the other man said while running and following his friends. I continued to free as many slaves as I could, and by the time, I had freed at least nineteen slaves while others were free from the gullies and cages, Drestoloy Frett started calling my name.

"Look, Perig, they've got the creature," he said. I looked over and ducked by the husk of a broken boat. I could hear high pitched screams and shrieks made by the creature and then cries from the men. I got up to see if they were okay, but unfortunately the creature launched toward me, arms outstretched, ready to claw out my throat, but in the nick of time, she recognised me as I did her.

***

We rested the night and returned the following night to the market town of Humt al Suk. "This is Nene. I met her in the mountains two months ago," I said, introducing Nene, the hybrid, to Maya and the rest. Nene stood still with her child clung to her. She had apparently followed me when I left their cave and hid in the market but was captured by slavers.

"Well, she sure is one driggle-draggle," said Drestoloy Frett.

"Ugh?" replied Nene.

"This man is a hero, Maya. Why don't you go ahead and tell him why you really came here," said Drestoloy Frett. Maya looked at me and sighed and then gave out a little smile and said, "I kept having these strange dreams, Perig. This girl with flowers kept telling me to come here. I just feel like I should be here with you."

"Dreams, huh?"

Chapter 15: Ibn Arabi

"Our investigations reveal that it was the Kohanim that had arranged the break-in. They are the ones that stole the book Perig," said Tahir.

"What a turn of events. Are you sure?"

"Yes, positive, some of their own told us the book is there with them. They are studying it," replied Tahir. He continued, "Please sit down, Perig, let's talk."

"Right, sure," I sat down next to Tahir on an intricately patterned carpet laid on top of a mat. We sat looking out to the sea, facing each other only slightly. Tahir had just returned from a swim at sea. The compound was large and stood on slightly higher ground. I could hear his students reciting verses from ancient scripture while a graceful wind blew in my face.

"My wife will bring you refreshments if you want."

"No, I'm okay, she doesn't have to."

"Should we send some of our students to retrieve the book? The Kohanim felt they had to use that approach, but they are still priests. If confronted, they will give the book back," asked Tahir.

"No, let them have it," I said, realising they were probably the only ones that stood a chance at deciphering the Book of Gnosis. "So quick question, if the Muhammadans, Catholics and *Yahudim* all get their 'laws' from the same source, why all the animosity?" I asked, "And I know these are not really laws because laws are unchangeable by man. These are just customs. I've been told that before."

"The Muhammadans differ from the Catholics in that we don't worship any graven image. All we do is seek enlightenment. The Romans are confused," replied Tahir with a smile.

"So, returning to the topic of Ibn Arabi, I need to learn more about the Merkabah. I was told that one can use the Merkabah and crystal to travel or teleport from point A to B," I said.

"Mmm, first of all, Perig, that's very difficult. Let me tell you about the Crist."

"You mean Iesus? Yeshua, the one the Romans worship? My friend Samu was arrested by inquisitors in Toledo a few months ago because he went around town telling people that Iesus is allegorical or a spirit and never a real living breathing person." I said.

"Verily! Your friend speaks of *Ruhul-Quddus*—the Holy Spirit—. The problem with the western Romans is that they just want to control people," he said, then pointed at a herd of sheep, "you see them over there, if you create a simple system of pulleys that drive a conveyor belt which delivers food to the sheep and you let them graze openly, they will be free and independent. Only returning to the contraption to receive food, but if you feed them by yourself, they become nervous and fearful, unwise and dependent on the shepherd. That is akin to what the Romans have done, the whole world used to know about *Ruhul-Quddus*, but now they follow idols— *taghut*— ."

"Interesting, how can I meet the spirit?"

"The spirit is the air you breathe, so spirituality is the art of breathing. If you breathe properly, the spirit will contact you."

"Hmm, so what exactly did Ibn Arabi see?"

157

"Slow down, Perig, listen carefully, we have all afternoon. Let us understand a few things clearly because a web of lies and misinformation has to be unwoven first, and it's all tied to this man, Al Arabi," said Tahir. He adjusted his sitting position so that he faced me, and I did the same. "Please go ahead, Tahir," he then looked in the distance and began.

"I told you before that my grandfather named Al' As was one of the companions of Al Arabi. Basically, the name Arabi was given to the sheikh, his real name was Muhyī al-Dīn ibn ʿAlī, and in the Roman world, they referred to him as Doctor Maximus, said Tahir.

"So, where did he get the name Arabi?"

"Very good question. Arabi means 'of arab', or from arab."

"And what does that mean? A rabbi in the city of Al Fustat told me a few years ago that it meant teacher of the Merkabah. It doesn't sound too convincing, though and isn't a nation of people called that too or a language?" I asked, at which moment Tahir's very kind wife brought juicy sugarcanes from Darfur, and I grabbed one. "Funny you mentioned rabbi, rabbi means master and arab means master too. It used to be spelt with an 'alif', but now it is spelt with an 'ain'. I suspect a deliberate occlusion of its historical origin. So the word 'arabi' as a name is simply a designation

158

of the sheikh's mastery, that's why he is called Maximus in Europa, which means greatest or master of masters."

"I hear you, Tahir, but I have seen an entire village of people calling themselves 'Arabs' in a place near Al Fustat."

"That is very possible, the people could simply be followers of Ibn Arabi, who are probably following the teachings closely or just followers of a particular teaching of the Merkabah."

"So the term will be like a religious appellative?"

"It might evolve to that, or it might evolve to become a 'name of a nation' of people who resemble Ibn Al Arabi in language or culture. He was of the Tayyi tribe."

"Or worse, he might come to be worshipped," I commented.

"That I fear most," replied Tahir, his eyebrows grew closer momentarily, and then he smiled and continued, "I see your friends have found a hybrid somewhere. There aren't too many of them left. They used to roam all around here when I was young."

"Oh yes, I found them high up in the mountain, and this one followed me."

"Very good, you see the Hellenes used to refer to the troglodytes as *erembi*, and the Etruscans called them *arabo*, but that's got nothing to do with Ibn Arabi," he said, looking at me while I smirked a little.

159

"I see…" I said, still not sure whether or not I accepted what Tahir was saying, all I wanted to know was how to do what Ibn Arabi and Rabbi Yishmael and Rabbi Akiva ben Yosef did. How can I see for myself if all of it was real. I was beginning to wonder if Ibn Arabi was even real or not. "Please tell me about the Crist."

"So Ibn al Arabi was drawn to God after his vision of Iesus when he was a child. You see, the *Ruhul-Quddus* or the Holy Spirit found him since he was a child. That's why I told you, Perig, even you… you are not ordinary. Please be calm and see, the Spirit will find you. Don't haste."

"Is that the same as the angel Metatron?"

"Ahaa *Mīṭaṭrūn,* all these are just names, whether you call it Jibril, Iesus or Michael, it doesn't matter. Angels are just light, and light travels in angles hence the name. They bring you the divine message," responded Tahir, his eyes glaring wisely.

"Oh, tell me more," I said, at which point it started to make sense to me.

"This is his book right here called the Al-Futūḥāt al-Makkiyya or the Makkan Illuminations," said Tahir as he turned a page.

"So, what does he mean by makkah?"

"Makkah is the Merkabah, it can also be pronounced as 'mer-kaba', or 'merca'. It means the 'light of the ka'ba'.

160

'Mer' means light. If you go to Eakuptah to a new city called Al Kahira —Cairo—, you will see *harim* or pyramids. Their real name should be mer, or 'per-neteru'—meaning house of light or house of nature."

"So the pyramids also symbolise the Merkabah? I remember seeing two pyramids in a temple at Taadamakkah, a town in the Empire of Mali. Now it's all making sense," I exclaimed in excitement.

"Yes, yes, yes, Perig, this knowledge is for you. I can see it," Tahir said with a stern look.

"So Tahir, tell me about the *Isra wal Miraj*—Night Journey—."

"I will tell you, but you need to know that people have already started editing his books, ascribing his personality to mythical figures that never existed. An example of such a claim is Ibn Tumart. The man is long dead, but recently some of his followers have tried to eulogise him by copying the life and works of Ibn Arabi and claiming that it is Ibn Tumart's work. However, what will be more dangerous is to fabricate a mythical character and place it farther back in time to make verifications even more difficult. I pray that doesn't happen."

"Isn't that what the Romans did with Iesus?"

"Yes, they are claiming a spirit actually lived on earth."

"So, just to clarify, Arabi was not a Catholic, right?"

161

"No far from it. The Catholics believe Iesus had a human body and lived on earth, but Ibn Arabi was philosophically a monist and in matters of Iesus a monarchianists— in other words, Iesus never was a man but a spirit."

"So Arabi had no other religion?"

"Religion is the reconnection to the divine, that's all it means. Hope that answers your question."

"So, where did he learn to be a monist from?"

"At the time in Madinat Mursiya, where he was born, many people except the Romance people were monophysites, so they didn't believe Iesus had a human body."

"What about his family?"

"His father was named Ali and was a carpenter, just like the story they made up about Iesus— the Holy Spirit—, they claim Iesus was also a carpenter. Ibn Arabi was gifted, he had an immense vocabulary and mastered many languages and wrote rhyming prose called *saj* before becoming an adult. He wrote a total of 800 books, and he had the purest heart. He learnt how to do *ta'wil* —interpretation— of dreams. Just like you, Perig, you are gifted with *ta'wil* too," he said.

"Did he have any teachers?"

"Yes, he did, one of which was Fatima bint al Waliyyah. He met her after he had declared that he had already become a prophet, but time is of the essence, Perig. The sun is far diminished. Let's talk about the prophet another day. For now, let us practice some of his teachings," replied Tahir, at which point he stood up and motioned for me to follow him.

***

We reached the beach later and were welcomed by a scenic view of the ocean illuminated by the magical glow which pervades the horizon at twilight.

"Alright, Perig, circumambulate the cube twenty-seven times, then use the door and go inside, lie down and prepare for the night journey, the *Isra*. As you lie down, imagine yourself going up a ladder, this is the *Mi'raj* or Jacob's Ladder," instructed Tahir excitedly.

"I will do that," I responded, determined more than ever to have the experience. "I have here with me…." Tahir paused to catch his breath in the windy evening, then carried on, "…the Kitab al Isra which is the book of travel written by Ibn Arabi. Ibn Arabi saw Adam in the sphere of the Moon, in the sphere of the Sun was Enoch, in the sphere of Venus was Joseph the beautiful, Mars had Aaron, in mercury was Iesus, Moses was in Jupiter, and Abraham was in Saturn."

My head was beginning to whirl from the circumambulation, and I recalled what happened years ago at Kukiya when I left my body, but then I had a high dose of Ibogaine. "Are those the spirits of the spheres?" I yelled.

"Yes, you may not necessarily see them with the names of those spiritual patriarchs, you might see something completely different. Each experience is unique. Don't panic, though," he advised.

"I think I just completed the twenty-seventh round," I blurted, my head slightly spinning, and I felt like lying down. There was also a mild pressure on the right-hand side of my head. "The right side of my head seems odd."

"Perfect, that feeling on the right-hand side of your head is the door-out, the doorway, the *Da'at* in Hebrew, *Duat* in the language of Eakuptah, and the *Barzakh* as understood by Arabi— that is the Eastern Gate where the soul leaves the body. Go into the *muka'ab*—cube—and lie down comfortably," instructed Tahir.

"Okay, I am inside. I am ready."

"Great, I will close the door soon. Come out whenever you are ready, no rush. Remember what you've studied about the breaths, that is, the true meaning of spirituality— the act of breathing-in the spirit or air—which will take you out through the door to God. Take seventeen breaths plus one. Good luck, my friend."

I felt my entire body encased in a warm sensation as I lay down in the darkness of the cube's interior, and then slowly, a warm, illuminating light began to appear in my mind's eye. I saw myself on a mountain top in the middle of the afternoon, and from all corners, as far as the eyes could see, were boats which kept rising as the sea level rose until the waters were easily reachable from the mountain top. The dream or vision was short and I woke up far into the night, slightly disappointed because I did not have an *Isra*—night journey—nor did I leave my body as I did years ago.

"Morning, Perig," said Tahir's wife as she passed the cube not too far from their backyard toward the sea. The door of the cube structure was ajar, and it seemed that Tahir must have left it open when he found me sleeping at night to allow for fresh air. I got up and hurriedly made my way toward her and asked, "Morning, where is Tahir?"

"He had to go into town early, just before dawn. He said you are from among the *Ahl-Kashf* —those who see with three eyes—. He said that whatever you see, please follow your heart."

Chapter 16: Journey to Mount Uwaynat

Over the next few minutes, I pondered on the vision carefully and recalled some key details that I had earlier missed, such as a voice in the background like a humming sound in my head which said— *'they are seven of them. You stand upon the biggest one. Go to the biggest, go east.'* I recalled that I was standing on a hill or mountain, and I could see other smaller mountains. *"Am I supposed to go to a mountain?"* I thought to myself, at which point I had lost touch with reality and did not even know why I was pursuing that path. It was not to help Samu anymore, but still, a burning desire raged inside me which could not be quenched.

The golden threads of morning light transformed my night's dream into an ambient optimism, and with a renewed purpose, I went to the guest house where Maya and her brother were staying to bid her goodbye. "Hello, morning all," I said. She was seated under a tree while another woman, who was a hairdresser, plaited her hair. "Hi, morning," they replied.

"I need to go somewhere, so I came to say goodbye."

"Where?"

"I'm not sure yet."

"What do you mean, you don't know?"

"I had a vision. I can't stay here. I need answers. I will come back for you," I said.

"No, I'll come with you then. I am not going to stay here," she protested adamantly. "And then?" I asked.

"Let's figure out where to next after we get back here. I am not saying you need saving, Perig. I just don't want you to do something without thinking it through."

"And your brother?"

"My brother is an adult, and he can take care of himself. When we come back, we shall all return to the Empire," answered Maya.

"To Mali? I don't know about that."

***

Several weeks passed while I planned for the journey. I travelled far and wide on the island of Girba, looking to find any information on where the 'seven' were but could not find anything worthwhile until one autumn evening when Drestoloy Frett returned from a fishing trip at sea.

"I have some good news, it might be a lead," said Drestoloy Frett.

"The sea was calm and placid so we had a lot of time just sitting. I had a conversation with some sailors. They mentioned a place to the north not too far from—" Drestoloy Frett did not finish speaking when Maya interrupted him,

"Why did you go out with the Hybrid's child?" she roared. Drestoloy Frett scowled at her and then removed his boots and sat on the ground of the sandy courtyard of the guesthouse that Maya had purchased, shook his head disappointingly and said, "What did we say about calling them hybrids? Please, not in front of the child."

"I know, I know, but you know Nene is very clingy with her son. You don't want her getting upset," replied Maya, reaching out to offer the child a fruit. He detested animal flesh despite some of the Hybrid's tendency toward the consumption of flesh—even cannibalism. "She let me take the child," replied Drestoloy Frett.

"I guess that's because she doesn't see you as a threat," I said.

"And why is that, wise guy?"

"Well, I guess because you are—"

"Oh, don't even go there. Are you trying to suggest that because I'm small?"

"No, I wasn't going to say—"

"So why does she see monkeys, cats, dogs, and even lizards as threats?"

"Gentlemen, please," hissed Maya intrusively, "and by the way, you guys shouldn't keep calling him the hybrid's child, we should call him something."

"Ahh! I say Uradech, that's a warrior's name. A name with a will," said Drestoloy Frett.

"You know, I was thinking since he hates eating flesh, why don't we call him Abū al-ʿAlā Al-Maʾarri? After the famous vegan philosopher?" I said.

"Okay, that is sensible, but I prefer the Latin version, it has a better ring to it— Abulola," responded Maya.

"Ahh, boring. He is a hybrid, not a philosopher!" bellowed Drestoloy Frett in remonstration. "Okay, how about 'Abulola Drestoloy', huh? You can give him your name as his surname," I said, bursting out laughing.

The grounds of the guesthouse had evolved into an unending babble of visitors coming from far and wide heading to a church that had been set up by Ghaly and Gethin in an old granary adjacent to the guesthouse. From within, melodious psalmody from monks could be heard as they recited canticles. At the entrance of the church, Ghaly had shown his artistic mastery in sculpture by erecting a statue of the Virgin and Child in a Romanesque rendition and in the corner of Nene, the hybrid and her child.

**

The very next day following Drestoloy Frett's lead we journeyed a short distance north by sea, arriving in the city of Qayrawan, which was exceptionally warm for that time of year. The cork oak trees blossomed, revealing the youngest green, their barks peeled to reveal a lighter brown colour, and catkins lent a pleasant yellow streak to the green and brown background. Farther still was the Mosque of Uqba— by far the most imposing structure in the city. I followed Drestoloy Frett and we arrived at a workshop of a polymath, slightly obscured by a wide array of vendors setting up kiosks.

"Good day, we came all the way from the island of Girba because we were told there is no rock you do not know of," said Drestoloy Frett to the man, who could barely see due to the rheum of age, though as compensation he had an extremely eidetic memory. "Please sit down, my eyes are not as they were, so I need these stones," he said, his wrinkly hands shaking as he pulled out a parchment. "What are those?" I asked.

"These are reading stones, they magnify the writing, I saw them in Cordoba. No one could replicate them since Ibn Firnas, the first man to fly; who also invented the stones. I studied tirelessly, and before the age of fourteen, I replicated all his inventions and more," said the man, and he could see the excitement in my person and my fatigue from the journey vanishing as swiftly as a bright Phoebean dart. "Wow, sir, that's inspiring, what more have you invented?" I asked.

"Well, for starters, that little midget is already over there playing with my planisphere…Haha," he crackled.

"Drestoloy, please be careful, don't break anything," I whinged.

"Oh no, let him have a look, I have many inventions."

"Okay, phew!" I replied and sighed with relief.

"So, what are you looking for?"

"We are looking for a place in the East where there are seven mountains," I tried to clarify Drestoloy Frett's earlier statement, but the old man did not seem to have caught on. "That is too vague, can't work with that," the old man griped.

"I had a vision, I was standing on a mountain, and a voice said there were seven hills, go to the biggest one, head east," I replied.

"Let me take out my map. This was drawn over thirty years ago, of Bilad Asudan. I flew over those lands with this contraption," the old man pointed at a mechanical device stored in his store, which could be worn like the wings of a bird. "Amazing!" I exclaimed.

"Alright, I'll tell you exactly where you'll find a collection of seven hills, but it depends on how far you are willing to go. Was it in a forest?"

"No grasslands but verging on desert."

"Great! That is very key information," he replied, his eyes scanning meticulously at his incredibly detailed map. I saw the Empire of Mali laid out accurately showing every lake, every tributary, and every hill, and I also saw Britain, the rivers, the villages, and even Newgrange, and then his finger came to an abrupt stop and rested gently on a location on the map, south-west of Eakuptah. He looked up, moving the reading stone from his eye, and said, "These might be your rocks—Jabal Babein, Jabel Nazar, Jabal Arkenu, Jabal Bahari, Jabal Kissu, Jabal Kamil, and Jabal Uwaynat– their biggest."

"Oh my God, what a strange man you are, Perig. You just can't make this up," chimed Drestoloy Frett.

"It's a barren wasteland, tread carefully. I bid you good luck," said the old polymath and gently rolled out of sight on a chair that had wheels.

***

One week later —after having returned to the Island of Girba to take Maya along— , we arrived at the fertile delta of the Nile, at the ancient city of Rhakotis —renamed Alexandria by the Hellens— and then descended farther on to the Canopic River, one of the seven distributaries of the Nile. We disembarked the seafaring vessel that had got us that far and the captain moored it near a bouy called *shamandura* in the Nubian language. We then boarded a smaller frameless vessel fit for rivers, typical of the ones constructed in Nubia. The vessel was expertly piloted by Nubian boys who sang and chanted with drums as the boat gently glided on the river.

Finally, by the dawning of night, we reached the city of Qasr Ibrim —Palace of Hebrew—a city with a fort in lower Nubia and found a large cathedral with Iesus iconography in its interior.

"Maya, we're staying here in this cathedral overnight," I said, "and tomorrow we start again."

"Oh, how much more? I am so seasick, and then this river is just never-ending," responded Maya wearily.

"I told you to stay behind with Nene and Abulola," commented Drestoloy Frett groggily, who then hurriedly found a mat made with camel swede and fell asleep as soon as we arrived, while Maya and I stayed out by the shores of the river at the steps of the cathedral. Across the river on the eastern bank was a large bonfire and sounds of festivities going on.

"You should go to bed, Maya. I have some exploring to do, it's still quite early."

"No, I shall tag along," she replied. We walked along the shore and saw small figurines made with wood, copper, and gold lined up along the shoreline of the river. We also witnessed singing and drumming, which reminded me of the night of the rites at Kukiya but not quite as intense. "What is going on here?" I asked an acolyte at the cathedral. "Tonight is *Lailat al Nuktah,"* replied the young acolyte. "Oh, I see, so why are you not participating?"

"Because the people are naked, we are not allowed to join them," replied the acolyte. "What is *Lailat al Nuktah,"* inquired Maya, but the acolyte was called to help move a chair indoors. Instead, the question was answered by a Lady who was leaving the cathedral. "It is the night of the drop. The teardrop of the goddess which causes the river Kush —Nile— to rise around this time every year."

"Oh, good to know," responded Maya. I left the two of them and ventured farther down the shore and saw a congregation of men chanting and dancing with drums while women on the side giggled and children looked on in amazement, but in the midst of all the jollification, there were some sounds of 'boo-hoo' and some long faces. "Why are they weeping?" I asked a passerby, who was too intoxicated to respond, I turned around and saw Maya trotting toward me very fast, "They will sacrifice a virgin in the Nile River. Let's leave right now, I don't want to see it," she demanded.

"Right now? But it's late."

"No, it's not late. We can still leave."

"We need to rest Maya. We have a long way to go tomorrow."

"Please, Perig, I'm going to go and wake Drest up and get the rest of the things," replied Maya, then began to pace back to the cathedral.

"Wait, let me come with you," I yelled. I went into the cathedral from its southern door, right next to the vestry, where a voice interrupted my stride. "You seem in a hurry, everything okay?" said a bishop.

"Yes," I replied.

"I saw your wife storming in just a few moments ago."

"She's not my wife... a friend."

"Does she want to leave already?"

"She is upset about the virgin sacrifice, why do you let it happen?"

"It is the seventeenth of June, that's why but we don't sanction it. We just can't stop it either. Not even the chief primate has a say in this."

"Oh my, that is too bad."

"Yes, it's been going on for centuries. It comes from the Mysteries of Isis, which come from the Eleusinian Mysteries. They will not stop anytime soon. Though things have improved."

"So, what are your beliefs here at the cathedral?" I asked the bishop.

"Our main primate is the head of the Coptic church in Alexandria. That is our creed. Though originally some of us were Miaphysites."

"So right now, you believe Iesus had a human nature, and he is not just a spirit?"

"Yes, I believe without a shadow of a doubt that Iesus began his ministry in the countryside of Roman Yudea with his Baptism by Yohanan the Baptist up until the last supper in Yerushalayim," he replied with a smile and then continued, "what you are saying is heresy. It is Docetism. Have you ever come across the heretical works of Gnosticism?"

"Okay, I take it back. Another question, are you Melkites?"

"No, it's fine, and yes, we ARE quite obviously Melkites because our beliefs are 'state-backed'. That is what 'melkite' means," he clarified, still with a smile on his face.

"Ahh so that is what Melkites mean: those who take the official religion from the king or state. Is it related to *Malikiyyah* in Syria?"

"Oh yes, the Syrians, both those who speak Syriac and those who speak Hismaic are bitterly Non-Chalcedonian *Malikiyyah*," he concurred.

"So toward the south in Alodia and in Abyssinia, they are *Milikiyyah*?"

"Yes, correct," he said.

"So why is this place called the Palace of Hebrew? Is it because you speak Hebrew?"

"Oh no, it's not that at all. My Hebrew is poor, as you can see. Rather the term Ibrim as used in a religious context — not ethnic—, means 'those from beyond the river' and that used to be part of an ancient ritual whereby the pilgrims would come to a riverside house like this and stay overnight and then cross the river by the first light. So it is just symbolic. Many houses by the river or temples coming from this tradition are called 'Palace of Ibrim' or the house of Hebrews. The city takes its name from this. Oh, look, here come your friends. It was nice chatting with you," he further clarified while bidding us goodbye with a very amiable expression.

Chapter 17: Journey to Mount Uwaynat

II

"Oh God, the sands are just unrelenting," fumed Maya, her eyes achy from lack of sleep and irritated by the piercing winds of the desert. Soon the last clouds of the season formed, offering slight relief from the burning sun but the heat still raged. "Oh, stop caterwauling, my dear Maya, though I see your pain, these grounds are not for maidens," responded Drestoloy Frett, who dismounted his camel and had been on foot since the last oasis. He was a very strong man despite his miniature size.

We spent days travelling in the wilderness, moving on camels from one oasis to another and sometimes navigating at night with the help of three bedouin teenagers who use the stars to find oases that can be used as a source of refreshment— especially for the camels. There were screeching sounds coming from eagles looking for desert scorpions, snakes or lizards. The descent of night offered no relief, the heat was simply replaced by a pervasive dry wind, chilling and sucking the juices out of all who dared to venture toward Mount Uwaynat. We reached a rocky valley with wind-worn rock formations and an oasis of acacia that formed at a natural spring called Ain Dua. The camels rejoiced and paced to drink and eat from the shrubbery that clustered around the spring. From the corner of my eye, I saw a date palm, but before I made my way toward the palm tree, one of the teenagers said, "Oh, do not bother. Those palms are dwarf palms of this valley, they offer no date fruits."

"Oh, I was looking forward," I replied, my lips all chapped and the corner of my eyes painful whenever I sweat due to tiny cuts caused by small grains of sand. "And by the way, this is where we leave you. We can't go any farther. Beyond, there is a village of the Tubu. None knows this wilderness as them," said the elder of the teenagers, and they turned around and left, easily disappearing into the vast brown of a background marred by sand.

We carried on for a short while and found the village of the Tubu —which had been abandoned for years— in a valley called Karkur Murr, where an oasis formed in a natural guelta. We rested there for a day and set up a camp. "I'm going to go up to the mountain," I said to Maya and Drestoloy Frett. Maya was immersing her feet inside a shallow pool while Drestoloy Frett was preparing food from the xeric plants that populated the oasis. Maya waved at me, too exhausted to speak, while Drestoloy Frett said, "Go but don't cry wolf. Only call out if you need help."

***

I began to climb the soaring massif in a slight fit of pique, my emotions swaying back and forth between self-doubt, self-pity, optimism, anger and excitement. There was I, going places on a whim and engaging in life-changing journeys. If I were alone, I would have been fine, but a part of me felt guilty for dragging my friends along, even though Maya insisted and Drestoloy Frett only went because of her. Before reaching very high up, I could see the whole massif morphing— from intrusive granite to sandstone, like a living being or a titan, petrified and castaway to spend an eternity prostrating in desolation. In the corner was an entryway, hollowed out by erosive winds over millennia and within and without stood gigantic hoodoos, towering in majestic glory. I reached one of the hoodoos and heard voices, I was taken aback and nearly lost my footing.

"While you were exploring, we also came here," said Maya, after having slept for a few hours. "Yes, have you gone far?" asked Drestoloy Frett.

"No, not really, I was looking at ancient glyphs on the walls of caves and rocks," I replied.

"This place is a time capsule," said Maya.

"Look, these are fairy chimneys," said Drestoloy Frett, pointing at the huge rock hoodoos. "There could be some fairies around, you know," he continued. I noticed fresh footprints on the ground, and then I moved around the hoodoo to take a look.

"It is indeed," a voice came, seemingly out of nowhere, it was Samu standing behind us. "Samu? How did you get here? I thought you were still in Guadix?" I asked, barely able to control my excitement.

"While you were working on finding your way here, I was also working on finding my way. I've been here for a week, and I knew you'd show up sooner than later. Come this way," he said, leading us down a narrow track which dissected rock outcroppings towards a valley. The whole place was labyrinthine without the help of the teenage Bedouin navigators, but Samu seemed to have mentally mapped the place already. He was wearing a Roman toga as though he were a pilgrim. "Why are you wearing a toga? And what about your turban?" I asked Samu, who had grown

181

out his hair over the period of a year that he had been in Toledo.

"I lost it in the wind. Unlike you, I did not come from the Nile. I could not avoid the desert as you did. I came straight through it, but with the help of a caravan. They are still here, hurry."

Upon reaching the valley, we saw a group of pygmies even smaller than Drestoloy Frett, ranging from about eighty-five to one hundred in number. They were led by a queen who was seated on a camel saddled with a finely crafted shelter which had a roof and veils. The group was composed of archers and men with axes, and there were also four regular-sized people as well as camels and dogs.

"So you came with them?" I asked.

"Yes, I did," replied Samu.

"They are so beautiful," said Maya and hurriedly went to their midst and started asking them questions. "I am Maya. Where are you from?" she asked, but they did not reply, instead directing Maya to their queen, who told Maya that they were originally from Schweizersbi in the frigid lands of the North but expanding races of man, emerging from the East had driven them south.

"The aged and the infirm among us could not travel too far, so they stayed in Fez," said the queen of the Pygmies, emerging only slightly from her shaded camel summit. Maya would later inform me that the queen had developed vitiligo and could not tolerate the sun.

"Where are you going?" asked Maya.

"We are going to Yam," replied the queen, who thanked Samu very much for his help, and he thanked them too for providing him with a hidden path to mount Uwaynat known only to the Bedouins, the hardened Tubu and the Pygmies.

"So, how did the Pygmies know this route?" I asked Samu as he led us to the cave he had been staying in while we bid the Pygmies goodbye. "The Pygmies know these paths very well, they are heading south to meet other pygmy tribes in the rainy forests, and beyond to the very south where beautiful temperate grasslands exist, as that is the climate they are used to," replied Samu, who started a fire inside a cave to prepare food. "There is a temperate clime to the south?"

"Yes, I have been there in my youth, and even beyond, it becomes frigid," he replied. I looked at Samu with wondrous eyes and realised that my curiosity had missed his wide array knowledge.

"Drest why are you so quiet," said Maya, "did you want to follow the Pygmies?" She addressed Drestoloy Frett jokingly, but he just looked on as the last of the Pygmies disappeared on the horizon under the receding sun. "Ha! Are you kidding me? Can you believe those little things? They looked at me as if I were a regular biggie," he responded.

"Biggie?" I asked.

"Yes, like you, you know a 'biggie-man' haha," he laughed.

***

Deep into the night, I woke up from a dream in which I saw a swarm of locusts blackening the sky in the afternoon. I looked around the cave and saw Samu sleeping near the embers of the small fire he had started earlier in the evening, and Drestoloy Frett was by the corner, but Maya was missing and at the entrance of the cave was a jackal-like animal. I immediately grabbed my sword and headed toward the animal to scare it off, but it did not move and instead remained there gnarling in a surly way. Drestoloy Frett got up and threw a rock at the jackal, hitting its tail, which made it run away. "It will be back," said Samu, "these are not harmful, they are hybrids that protect these rocks," he continued.

"Hybrids?"

"Yes, they were bred since ancient times."

"I'm going to look for Maya," I said and began to call her name out loudly, but there was no response. I went all around the paths we took earlier and even the heights I had earlier scaled but to no avail. By the time I returned, all three of us had begun to search for her. "What are they hybrids with?" I asked Samu.

"They were bred by the ancient people of Eakuptah, only they knew how to cross a domestic dog and the black-backed jackal."

"What are their purposes," a puzzled Drestoloy Frett, asked.

"Intelligence and obedience," replied Samu.

"Maya! Maya!" I yelled out, but my voice only echoed and grew hoarse. Only moments later did we hear Maya's voice from a platform a few metres above where the three of us were standing. "Over here," she said, calmly but excitedly. We tried to make our way up there through tight rock passes that spiralled upward. "Did you go up this way, Maya?"

"Yeah, right, she definitely did!" Drestoloy Frett deadpanned, rolling his eyes sarcastically. Samu was ahead and had reached a space so tight that he could not pass, so he offered to help Drestoloy Frett pass through. While the two of us found another path, finally arriving at a roundish door which served as a barricade for ancient dwellers of the cave or gorge. There were glyphs on the walls similar to those from ancient Eakuptah, and a large crystal in the centre of the rock-enveloped cave or gorge.

"What female eyes see, we do not see sometimes," chortled Samu.

I walked toward Maya, who was preoccupied, looking at the glyphs under the moonlight, which fell gracefully from the naturally hollowed out roof of the cave, making the large green crystal at the centre of the cave glow in a fulgurous way like I had never seen before. "This crystal does not look natural, it's almost as if it flickers," I commented. Below the crystal was a blackened material that had a molten effect as though it was flowing but had since frozen.

"You are correct, this cave was used by the Huskahs. My research into the Huskahs lead me first to the Pygmies and then here. I learnt that the Pygmies had known about the Huskahs but had kept it a secret for centuries," responded Samu.

"How did you find this cave, Maya? Are you okay?"I asked, but Maya seemed lost in awe, withdrawn and dazed, looking at a stony tabletop fashioned with granite and polished magnificently by ancient craftsmanship. The tabletop had inscriptions or petroglyphs detailing journeys of pygmies and regular people or 'biggies' as Drestoloy Frett would say. Further down the table were more petroglyphs showing sea animals that had been brought out of the water and made to live in the world of man. I saw the image of a woman adorned with seashells with no legs but having a lower body instead of a fish or some other sea creature. "Are these all just mythological?" I asked Samu.

"Yes, later cultures and travellers of all kinds who found a dwelling in this trans-Saharan nexus have drawn here what they fancied, but some inscriptions are not just folly," replied Samu as he looked up at a crevice in the walls of the open-top enclosure. "Yes, I'm okay, Perig. I just couldn't sleep because I slept in the afternoon. Besides, if I sleep, who will look out? There could be cheetahs and hyenas," Maya finally responded to my query about whether or not she was okay. She turned around and looked at the three of us and then continued, "so I left the other cave and found this, which is not only high up, but it also has a door that can be rolled to seal it up completely— with a bit of effort of course."

Samu then climbed the polished table and used his height to reach the crevice he had noticed earlier and discovered that it was man-made. "I think this is a keyhole or something," said Samu.

"The queen of the Pygmies gave me a key and said it's for a room if I can find it. See if it works," said Maya. She flung a necklace key toward me, and I grabbed it and handed it over to Samu, who struggled to insert the key into the hole. He finally inserted the key and turned it to the right, which made a faint sound, but nothing happened, so we thought it was perhaps not a keyhole. "Where is Drest?" asked Maya.

187

"Over here," he yelled back, his voice resounding off the surfaces of the granite complex. "And something smells so nice. Is that barbeque?"

Chapter 18: The Huskahs

"Ahh! That smell is coming from here. Come and feast," bellowed Drestoloy Frett. The aroma seemed to be emanating from the tiny keyhole that Samu inserted a key in earlier, but soon the smell was more than just a whiff— it seemed like the entire enclosure was exuding the smell of delicious herbs. We realised that it was already dawn and that we had been in the cave that Maya found for quite some time, distracted by the assortment of tools and decaying papyri that littered the sandy floor. "What are you cooking?" I yelled toward Drestoloy Frett, whose voice was coming from a parallel room, somewhere in the rocky maze, separated by thin sandstone walls, but we still could not get to him. "There is a small hole down toward the entrance," replied Drestoloy Frett, his voice still echoing. I looked around and found the small entryway, but only Drestoloy could fit in there.

"Hmm, this must be the door opened by the key," Samu drawled, trying to make sense of the contraption that caused the door to open. "Looks like there is another way here," said Maya. She left the cave and led us toward an elevated precipice and then down toward a steep edge. We squeezed through a small tunnel and then reached another round door similar to the one of the previous enclosure. All three of us pushed hard, but the door did not budge. "Stand aside. Let me try," I said. I put my legs against the round door and leaned on the wall, then pushed as hard as I could with my legs, but the hatch-like door only budged slightly— not enough for anyone to go through. "There are some gears here with ropes. They are worn out but try again. Perhaps putting this lever down would help," said Drestoloy Frett, his voice coming from behind the round door.

There were sounds of water flowing underground, and then the round door rolled open with minimal effort. Inside the room —which was also hollowed upwards toward the sky— were gears made with rocks and wood. "These are very simple pulleys and gears, but they work," I said.

"Yes, they are," replied Samu.

"I think pygmies used to live here," commented Maya.

190

"That is a verity Maya, and the key opened the tiny door, but it also lured a small gazelle, and it got trapped here in this device which punctured its neck with sharp crystals. So I had to cook it, hehe" said Drestoloy Frett, who had already begun serving the herbs and deer meat. The blood of the deer was collected in a large crucible and channelled towards a series of tiny canals around the cave.

At that moment, I realised the journey to Mount Uwaynat was not a wasted endeavour. It was highly rewarding, but still, my mind burned with the question of who or what the Huskahs were, and still, we had no clue. We sat down and had breakfast of the delicious deer meat and soup, except for Samu, who neither ate the flesh of the deer nor consumed the soup.

"I have another piece of evidence that pygmies lived here. Look, these leaves are yam leaves," said Maya, pointing at the leaves which spread on the ground and crawled on the walls of the cave upward toward the open sky.

"Wait a minute, didn't the Pygmies say they were going to the land of Yam?" I asked Maya.

"Yes," she answered.

"Yam?" said Samu. He stood up with a puzzled look, then continued, "I recall a story I heard many years ago about the people of Ancient Eakuptah trading with a people from Yam," recounted Samu.

"That means the people of Yam are pygmies," said Maya.

"How do you know?" I asked.

"Because I saw a petroglyph outside, in Eakuptahn language, mentioning the land of Yam," she replied.

"And not only that, if my suspicions are right, then the Huskahs lived with the people of Yam," said Samu. He then walked toward the sandstone walls of the enclosure and dusted off a surface of a cornered wall where he saw a petroglyph, but he could not make out what was written. "This is not the language of Eakuptah. This is a type of ancient Dongolawi. I don't know what it says."

"It says Huskahs," said Maya, "we used to study this when I was a child. We had many manuscripts from Makuria, but my brother is better than me at this."

"Impressive, Maya," I said.

"In that case, then, that device that the poor deer got trapped in is not for catching deers. It is for trepanation. This is some sort of research workroom," intoned Samu, his hand folded around his chin lightly while his eyebrows crossed in pensiveness. "Tra-pe—?" lisped and stuttered Drestoloy Frett. He rolled on the floor toward the device, "you mean this was used to open people's heads?"

"It gets worse. I found a few documents in a small royal library in Grenada when I was trying to find answers about the crystal. I think this crystal is even more harmful than the one we encountered in Kukiya, including the one in the adjacent room," said Samu.

"Could that explain why it has a fulgurous glow?" I added.

"And that explains why the yam leaves are gigantic," commented Maya.

"The Ancient Eakuptahns revered pygmies. Pygmies enjoyed high social status at the time of the kings and queens of Eakuptah. They called them *Deneg.* They were almost worshipped," said Samu.

"Why?" I asked

"Have you heard them sing? They are genius," replied Maya.

"Yes, I did in a vision," I replied.

"Look over here," Drestoloy wheezed and then sneezed, "I found something. It's a vase," he passed over a vase from a tight corner.

"Brilliant, let me take a look," said Samu, "oh, it's too encrusted in the earth. It's almost petrified. Let's get out of here before we catch influenza."

***

The rocks scattered around the guelta shimmered in the heat of midday as the sun climbed to its zenith. Tiny specks of dust suspended in the air appeared like a warm heavenly white light, creating an opaque veil to the outside world from our shaded retreat in the watery oasis. We left the caves above and sat at the oasis to have relief from the blazing sun. Drestoloy Frett joked that he would have been a lord in Ancient Eakuptah. Maya was lying down and almost drifting to sleep while I was beginning to look around for the best route to leave Mount Uwaynat. I scouted the site, and nothing stood out in the background except for a distant rocky tower which poked into the otherwise flat horizon.

"They were using the room above to create Huskahs," said Samu after a long period of silence. "How?" I asked.

"This whole complex was used for scientific breeding of all sorts. Not only were they mixing the domestic dog with the black-backed jackal, but they were also mixing humans with hybrids and others to create the Huskahs," said Samu assertively while continuing to clean the vase with water and a little twig which he used to scrape off the coagulated soil to read the glyphs on the vase.

"So the Huskahs were created? By who?"

"According to the information on this vase, they were originally from across the Ethiopian Sea. They came here to seek the tetrahedron. Some of them were hybrids, while some were more human. A son of theirs ventured northeast to the land of Eakuptah and became king, but he was ousted because he preached that sunlight could be spoken with," responded Samu, concentrating on the tiny glyphs etched on the vase. "Wow, that's amazing," I said, reaching over to take the vase from Samu. I raised it up, and it caught the light of the sun that penetrated through gaps in the rocks, which intensified the rays, making it flicker in Maya's face and waking her up to say, "I learnt about this when I was little, there was a king called Ekhnatan who came from a land in the West, and he had an elongated skull."

"Is that so... there are glyphs of people with elongated skulls here," I said, lowering the vase down and handing it back to Samu. "Did you say elongated skulls?" asked Samu.

"Yes, look at the bottom of the vase. Is that why you have a slightly elongated skull, Samu, because of your Huskah blood?" I joked.

"I know a place where people have elongated skulls, though theirs isn't natural but induced. It's south of here, deep in the forest," he replied.

"That must be the land of Yam that the Pygmies went to!" concluded Drestoloy Frett.

***

Early in the evening, we returned to the cave where Samu had been staying. We avoided the twin caves we had found earlier because Samu cautioned that the crystals were harmful.

"So Samu, how were they making the Huskahs?"

"I believe they were using the powers of Ra to make pregnant women give birth to children with elongated skulls. They needed the head to have a lot more cranial capacity compared with regular humans," replied Samu.

"The powers of Ra?"

"Yes, radium. That is what is inside the crystals."

"So the crystals are man-made?"

"That is correct. When radium leaks, it blackens from white. That is the viscous black substance you noticed."

"And it is harmful?"

"Very harmful."

"We need to leave this place tomorrow, and I'm concerned about the camels too. There could be predators here. I don't think those so-called 'guardian' hybrid dogs will protect them, or even us for that matter," Maya pointed out while preparing her sleeping bag made with hay and cotton, encased in sheepskin.

"You are right," all three of us replied in unison.

"So, what is this radium?"

"It comes from something else called uranium. Radium was in the first crystal we found at Kukiya. That is why the queen does not touch it, and that is why it caused me to develop dermatitis when I wrapped it on my back for a prolonged period of time," replied Samu.

"My mother knows about the crystals?" asked Maya. She reclined and yawned, gradually being overtaken by sleep. I looked at her and admired how she and Drestoloy Frett had an uncanny ability to easily fall asleep while I would still be wide awake.

"Yes, Maya, it appears she did know," I replied.

"So why weren't the crystals harming the Huskahs?" Maya somnolently exclaimed, this time falling asleep.

"I believe that would have led to the extinction of the Huskahs. I don't have enough information to know exactly if the crystals with the radium led to their demise or if it was something else," whispered Samu with a low tone so as not to wake Maya and Drestoloy Frett up.

"So what was the point of the whole experimentation to create Huskahs?" I asked Samu.

"If you recall the bodies of the Toloy pygmies we saw at Bandiagara Escarpment, they had a huge round head. I believe they were mixed with regular humans to create the Huskahs. A larger brain meant more mental capacities. I suspect their third eyes were much larger than ours, so they could see clearly with their mind's eyes," responded Samu.

197

"Hmm, so that is what seeing with three eyes means," I added.

"Indeed, it's all about mutations to create a human that could see the other world," said Samu.

"So it's about evolution and religion?" I asked.

"Yes, it's about religion in the sense that all that humans seek —to connect with God or to experience the higher self— is based upon their inability to do so naturally without rituals and repetitions," replied Samu.

"So the pygmies can connect with God better or experience the higher self or communicate with the Holy Spirit?"

"The pygmies have a simple temperament, which is usually sanguine. They are always positive. Because of their small stature, they tend to be child-like. The Huskahs combined that in order to have the best of both worlds. I mean, the Huskahs were tall. They were at least eight feet five inches on average," replied Samu.

"From what I recall from Bandiagara Escarpment, the Toloys had huge heads, like you just mentioned. What sort of mental prowess do you think they possessed?"

"With a brain like that, which was at least, at least, sixty per cent bigger than ours, they would have done wonders. Keep in mind the ratio of their brains to the rest of their bodies. They would have been able to easily control the minds of creatures around, but possibly even possess the ability to disappear and reappear at will and create the technology we can only dream about," replied Samu.

"They were fairies," said Drestoloy Frett, who had apparently been listening.

"So the Huskahs were man's attempt at evolving, but they were possibly killed off by the toxicity from the radium?"

"Probably," replied Samu.

Chapter 19: Above it is Nineteen

"Where is Maya? Please, I need to find her, now," I asked, exacerbated. I must have been going around for at least half an hour. "Good morning, the viscountess? This way, sir," a middle-aged man answered and motioned for me to follow him. He led me through the hallways of an ornately decorated palace with soft silky carpets on the floor. I looked down and realised I wasn't wearing shoes, and I was dressed in a winter garb of the highest quality. There were pictures with golden frames hanging on the walls. "Can I sit down? I'm tired," I sat down on a chair in a sitting room which was adjacent to the hallway.

"I'll get her. You rest here," the man said, returning to the hallway and closing the door behind him. The windows of the large parlour lined up with the high ceiling all the way down to the floor of the room. Fresh breeze blew from vents built into the ceiling— a show of architectural prowess in a way that air was channelled from outside. I stood up after resting a little bit, opened an opposite door to the one I used to get into the room, and it led to a sunny but windy garden, where a curly-haired middle aged man with a built body sat on a bench. He smiled at me and said, "For indeed, as you also say, life is a grievous thing. For I should not wonder if Euripides spoke the truth when he says: 'Who knows whether to live is not to die, and to die is not to live?' And perhaps we are, in reality, dead. For I have heard from one of the wise that we are now dead; and that the body is our sepulchre; but that the part of the soul in which the desires are contained is of such a nature that it can be persuaded and hurled upward and downward."

"What? Are you talking to me?" I replied, but he just stared at empty space. By then, I began to run, and I went straight back to the parlour and opened the door toward the hallway, but the door opened to a medium-sized room instead, where I saw Maya standing, dressed in a beautiful dress with flowers on her head. She was surrounded by three women who were dressing her up, getting her ready for an event. "Please, sir, you are not supposed to see the bride just yet," said a young lady, ushering me back out of the room.

***

The next few moments were blank. I floated mindlessly in a vast emptiness, a vast void of nothingness except a buzzing monotone sound which lingered infinitely until it was abruptly muted and the scene dramatically altered. I felt a dampness on the sole of my feet. I felt the fibrous texture of grass. I felt the distinctive clammy nature of loamy soil under the grass, the blackness began to dissipate from my eyes, and I could see again. I saw trees, a thick forest and the smell of tropical undergrowth. I looked up in the sky and saw a familiar collection of stars, it's Dhanab al-Dajājah, or the

201

constellation of Cygnus. I yearned for the stars, and in their midst, I was. It was bright, too bright to see. The refulgence of the stars altered my vision, making me see with a tinge of luminous green colour and a touch of blue. The stars were warm to the touch and smelt of flowers. The light of the stars travelled straight down to the land, and I slid down on their rays with an immense feeling of joy and familiarity— like I had done it hundreds of times before. I was no longer afraid or scared. I reached a point directly above the lands, which formed a geometric pattern.

Suddenly the sky was bright, and the sun appeared, shining its light through the geometric shape above the earth, thereby causing life on earth to emerge. I saw the earliest plants besprinkled over the plains of earth and the earliest beasts roaming the lands. I then saw a time when gigantic humans laboured, creating gardens of splendour and another time, an era of the Huskahs when pygmies had kingdoms in the clouds. Finally, I saw the lands of earth merged together, forming a triangular shape and beings of light living harmoniously in cities of indescribable beauty, but a large earthquake cracked the triangular landmass, which caused the once encircling waters to violently flood the lands. The ensuing disaster caused cracks in the joints of the landmass, which eventually led to a breakage of the land. The beings of light then solidified into rocks. Fierce winds raged, creating frost, which caused the sun to die and a period of darkness followed for over a thousand years. Finally, a new light came from the ground. A fiery orange glow of molten material ran around the earth and took the place of the waters of the earth. It was hell, populated by demoniacal creatures, and above the hellish earth, were nineteen beings of light who patrolled the infernal Hadean world.

For a moment, I felt a streak of sorrow, but then my mind buzzed positively and alacritously. I saw Samu, Drestoloy Frett and Maya standing beside me. "Are you okay?" asked Maya with worried eyes. "Yes, I'm okay. What's wrong?" I asked.

"You have been zoning out since we came to Yam," said Samu.

"This time around, you were in dreamland for two days," said Drestoloy Frett.

"Two days?" I replied.

"I suspect prolonged exposure to the crystals. I felt the same way in Guadix," said Samu.

"Okay, great to see all of you, but I have some questions. How did we get to Yam all the way from Mount Uwaynat?" I asked all three of them, but none of them answered except Drestoloy, "Boats?"

"Hmm, listen, I had all these visions—"

"Don't worry; we found Yam. The pygmy queen knows a lot about the crystals. She can help you," said Maya.

Yam was a beautiful city built with tiny bricks and at its centre was the queen's castle of moderate size with emerald and ruby roofing. We reached the entrance of the castle, which had stairs with nineteen steps leading to the door and then a space to walk and followed by two more steps, making a total of twenty-one steps.

"So, is this place south of Mount Uwaynat?"

"Yes, this is very much south. It's the land of abundance, so much food and many more indulgences," replied Drestoloy Frett.

There were pygmies everywhere of various stocks from all over the world. It was a pygmy sanctuary. We opened the door of the queen's castle, which led to a hall of walls which formed concentric circles— beautifully furnished with statues of golden rhinos.

"So, where is this place?" I asked.

"It is near Ga Mohana, the city of crystals where it all began. It is near the great Kingdom of Mapungubwe —the Hill of Jackals— where our brothers from the East have been mining gold for over a millennium," replied the queen, her voice coming from a hole in the wall. "Why can't we see her?"

"She doesn't allow anyone to see her," replied Maya.

"Queen, excuse my curiosity, but I have many burning questions," I asked.

"Perig, please ask her to cure you, not more useless questions," barked Maya angrily. She heaved and folded her arms while I struggled to understand her behaviour. "No, let him ask. The questions will help him. Please go ahead and ask," said the queen.

"Firstly, why is Ga Mohana the beginning?"

"Ga Mohana was used over one-hundred thousand years ago by the early ones who did not have the top part of the head that we do. Their use of the crystals is what brought us about. This is because the cosmic rays from the bird—Cygnus—were absorbed and intensified by the crystals."

"Okay, I know what you are talking about—evolution. I had an out of body experience. I saw nineteen beings of light above a fiery pit. Is that hell? And what are the beings of light above it?"

"The beings are us. This is the realm of nineteen. Our ancient ancestors at Ga Mohana who did not have the top of the head were in the realm of eighteen or consciousness of eighteen."

"Staggering, so they were like the hybrids on the mountains of the kingdom of Ifriqia?"

"Something like that. Now Perig, in the past, some pygmies have evolved so incredibly to the twenty-one level

205

of consciousness as known in Ancient Eakuptah. Those pygmies were worshipped as gods."

"So, where are they now?"

"Sometimes, you can catch a glimpse of them. They are grey and live in hyperspace or the Otherworld."

"So what is the point of trying all these things, I mean religion? Since a future version of ourselves is already evolved?"

"Because, if you don't, you will experience the lower realities and never the higher," interjected Samu.

"That is correct," said the queen. The queen emerged from behind a wall with a veil over her face and botched makeup covering the patches on her pale arms from vitiligo. She went up a set of stairs and sat on her throne. The Pygmies then began to sing and offered us refreshments.

"If you are feeling better, we need to leave. We can't just keep travelling from point A to B. What about our lives elsewhere?" said Maya, still fuming.

"I have more questions. Please be patient, Maya," I said. I saw Drestoloy Frett seated on the polished floor of the queen's castle and Samu by the door. I gestured toward Maya to calm down, and then I approached the queen's throne and asked another question. "I keep having blackouts. Can you cure me of the harmful effects of the crystal?"

"The crystal you touched is not natural and has something very harmful inside it. That is not how it was done in Ga Mohana. Luckily there are remedies which I will tell you about later. Any other questions?" said the queen while squinting her eyes wisely and clasping her nails together.

"Yes, you said your brothers from the East were mining gold at Mapungubwe?"

"Yes, their elders speak a moribund language—they are the last of their kind. They came from beyond the seaport of Tarshish."

"Is this a sanctuary for pygmies?"

"Yes, our last stronghold. If this falls, only the forests can protect us," she replied, her voice trembling a little. "So, where is this place exactly?"

"This is near Sofala, and I am the queen of Pygmies but also a *nhume* or ambassador of the Kingdom of the Lusvingo."

"Sofala? How did we get here in two days? All the way from Mount Uwaynat? It would have taken us at least two weeks to reach the *Yam Suph* or the Red Sea and then at least one month to reach here. I've seen Sofala on the map."

"Focus, Perig. You must have blacked out. How else would you explain being here in Yam?"

"I don't know. Anyway, why do you think you are safe here?"

207

"We pygmies are engaged in the gold trade here. We know the mines of Mapungubwe very well, and we can enter even the tiniest ones."

"Did you dig the mines?"

"Yes, we did, but with the help of the now ascended grey pygmies who have evolved."

"Enough with these questions! Why do you keep answering him?" screamed Maya. She banged on the wall and stamped her foot on the floor in a paroxysm of anger, much like a toddler. "Restrain her!" Said the queen. I tried to calm Maya down, but the guards gestured that the queen was not finished. Out of respect, I remained seated near the queen. There was a sharp pain at the back of my head, and my vision began to blur. "Are you okay?" asked the queen. "Yes, I'm alright, just a little headache." The queen left her post and instructed the Lord Chamberlain to allow guards to lower the curtains above the stairs. Behind the curtains was a mural showing the heavenly spheres above the Earth and the pits of hell below. The queen showed me the orbs one by one, but something strange happened when I saw the orb of Venus, which contained the image of a woman trapped and struggling to find her freedom. I went closer and realised that it was Maya trapped in the orb of Venus. "How did Maya get there? Who put her there? Where is the real Maya?" I asked.

"She led herself there," replied the queen. I then saw Cunedda, the king of Gwynedd, in the orb of Mercury. He smiled at me and turned around to continue with what occupied his mind. *"How is the queen creating this effect?"* I thought to myself. "Concentrate Perig, this is no effect," she said, appearing to have read my mind.

"Why am I seeing images in the mural, and all of a sudden, they move like magic?"

"Concentrate on the upper part of the mural," she replied, holding a long stick. She tapped on the upper part of the mural, where a heavenly light was shining brightly. "This is where you need to be so that the cracks can mend. The lands will reattach, the waters will recede back to their fons et origo, the Earth shall return to its original path of 360, the man shall not be separate from the woman, and the mindless beast shall return to the womb. Only this will stop the molten hell from emerging through the cracks that yet persist. You have now seen it. You can now help. Teach mankind that only love can take them to the top of the mountain."

"But I didn't tell you about that. How do you know about that vision?"

"Come this way. Look at this. I can only show you more evidence," replied the queen. I followed her through a hallway which had many doors. We entered the nineteenth door in which the stars floated below us. There were chains and gears of fire attached to the sun, which steer the sun on a fixed path upon the plain of the Earth, but some of the chains were no longer attached, and so the sun no longer followed its correct path. The moon was also anchored by a similar mechanism. "What's all this? How are we here?"

***

"Papa, papa."

"What? Who are you?"

"Papa, it's me, let's go, let's go," said a little boy no more than three years of age. "Morning, honey," I heard Maya's voice from beyond the boundaries of the room. "Maya!" I called out, "when did we get back? When did we leave Sofala?"

"First name basis?" she replied.

"Where am I?"

"We are in Britain."

"What? What about Drestoloy Frett?"

"He is not here. He's at home, I guess."

"What about Samu?"

"Who?"

"Samu, we were together in the Empire of Mali, and we went to so many places together. Don't you remember?"

"You need to rest, dear."

"What? You can't tell me you don't remember that!" I grabbed Maya's shoulders and shook her slightly. "Do you remember Mali?"

"Yes, I do."

"So?"

"Papa, papa, there's someone here to see you," said the little boy.

"Who?"

"A very tall man."

THE END

Lightning Source UK Ltd.
Milton Keynes UK
UKHW042214120622
404312UK00001BA/1